The Four Beauties
and the Four Beasts

FROM THE SAME AUTHOR

The Discovery of the Austral Continent by a Flying Man
ISBN 978-1-61227-512-3
Posthumous Correspondence (3 vols.) ISBNs 978-
61227-513-0; 514-7 & 515-4.
*The Story of the Great Prince Oribeau (Ouroucoucou –
1)* ISBN 978-1-61227-601-4

The Four Beauties and the Four Beasts
(The Fay Ouroucoucou – 2)

by
Nicolas Restif de la Bretonne

Translated, annotated and introduced by
Brian Stableford

A Black Coat Press Book

ISBN 978-1-61227-602-1. First Printing. March 2017. Published by Black Coat Press, an imprint of Hollywood Comics.com, LLC, P.O. Box 17270, Encino, CA 91416.

TABLE OF CONTENTS

Introduction

This volume contains the first two of six *contes bleus* [marvelous tales] that Nicolas Restif de Bretonne wrote over a period of approximately ten years, all of them featuring *La Fée Ouroucoucou*—the spelling of whose name Restif eventually began to render as Wrwcwcw—an onomatopoeic rendition of the call of an owl (or, strictly speaking, two owls), normally rendered in English as *too-wit-too-woo*.

The novella and the short novel included here were the first two stories in the series to be published; they appeared as interpolations in *Le Nouvel Abeilard*, one of Restif's ripostes to Jean-Jacques Rousseau, which borrowed the format of the latter author's *La Nouvelle Héloïse* (1761), in order to dissent from the educational theories he had expressed in *Émile* (1762). The first of the two stories is given the title of "Le Demi-Coq" in the margin of the original text and the second "Les Quatre belles et les quatre bêtes," which I have translated as "The Demicock" and "The Four Beauties and the Four Beasts."

Le Nouvel Abeilard appeared in four volumes in 1778-89, published in Paris by the widow Duchesne; the first of the two stories translated in the present volume is contained in two widely-separated sections in volume two, and the other, again in two separated sections, the first in volume two, in between the two sections of the first tales, and the second in volume three. Both narratives are continually interrupted in the original text by questions and comments made by the notional listener

7

and occasionally by external events requiring the fictitious narrator to pause; this is probably the first time that either story has been presented as a continuous and coherent narrative. The stories might have been written in the manner presented here, perhaps earlier than their insertion into the longer work—following a habit that was to become increasingly pronounced in Restif's more idiosyncratic works, some of which became eccentric patchworks of disparate materials—but there is no way to be sure, and the text of the second part of the longer story is not entirely consistent with the earlier section.

One of the most bizarre of those patchworks is the work into which three of the other four stories featuring the fay Ouroucoucou (I have translated "fée" which means "enchantress," as "fay" rather than "fairy," as it is often crudely translated in English works) were introduced as interpolations: *Les Veillées du Marais, ou, Histoire du grand Prince Oribeau, Roi de Mommonie, au pays d'Evinland & de la vertueuse Princesse Oribelle, de Lagénie; tirée des anciennes annales Irlandaises.* [Evenings in the Marais; or, The Story of the Great Prince Oribeau, King of Mommonia, in the country of Evinland, and the Virtuous Princess Oribelle of Lagenia; extracted from the ancient annals of Ireland], published in four volumes in 1785, and wholly translated, in a companion volume to the present one, as *The Story of the Great Prince Oribeau.*

The final version of the last of the stories featuring the fay in question is the main narrative of that longer work—which contains various other interpolations of different kinds as well as the three *contes bleus*—but some secondary sources allege that a short version of it had been published previously as a supplement to the second edition of *La Confidence nécessaire* in 1779 in which the central character had been called Prince O-Ribo. There is some doubt as to whether that book actually exists—the Bibliothèque Nationale only has the first edition of 1769—but if it does, there is no copy available for consultation. References in other works by Restif, however, offer some details as to the contents of the story of O-Ribo and suggest that it had first been written in or before 1775, although the final version must have undergone a very considerable rewriting, which changed its essential nature completely. The three interpolated stories, "Mellusine", "Sireneh" and an item untitled in the portmanteau work but referred to elsewhere as "La Fée Ouroucoucou," were almost certainly written considerably earlier than 1785, and inserted into the narrative of the novel, with certain modifications to adapt them to their new context.

The sequence of the six stories, and the peculiar manner of their publication, is interesting because it illustrates an awkward problem that Restif had—or thought he had—in producing *contes bleus* and offering them to an audience in what was supposed by the contemporary intelligentsia to be an Age of Enlightenment. The literature of past eras was, of course, replete with *contes bleus*, but they had long been regarded with some suspicion, as tales perhaps fit to tell to children but not suitable fare for intelligent adults, for whom belief in their fantastic apparatus was impossible. That had not stopped eighteenth-century writers from producing such tales in abundance, including some of the contemporary writers that Restif admired more than any others, but they had mostly used the strategy of presenting their fantastic devices as satirical exaggerations requiring sophisticated decoding in order to perceive their intended meaning. Restif was not averse to that—indeed, he could not resist the temptation, even in the course of stories that set out with a different agenda—but he felt that it distorted the element of the marvelous that made such stories attractive in the first place in a way that robbed it of its naïve impact.

Restif had been born Nicolas Rétif in 1734, the son of a farmer, in the vicinity of Sacy in the Yonne, the region in which the two stories in the present volume are both set, although some of the place-names are transfigured. He was sent away from home to further his education, and only returned briefly before embarking on a career, when he was apprenticed to a printer, but he always retained a strong emotional attachment to it. The "La Bretonne" that had added to his pseudonym in order to give it a quasi-aristocratic gloss was the name of a field owned for a while by his father, and he retained a similarly ironic pride in having once worked as a shepherd. In fact, he frequently referred back, in the autobiographical elements that he incorporated into his novels—in a lifelong quest to "lay bare the human heart" by using himself as an example for analysis—to a fellow shepherd who used to narrate local folktales to him while they were watching the sheep graze. His own *contes bleus* deliberately attempt to capture something of the effect that hearing those tales had on his young self. Indeed, elements of some of the particular tales that he was told are probably recycled in his own stories, albeit massively transfigured, and when he refers to the shepherd in question in his writings he sometimes calls him François or Francillon Courtcrou, linking him phonetically with the Fée Ouroucoucou.

There is no way of knowing whether Restif ever told *contes bleus* to his own children, but the fact that his wife Agnès had four daughters in rapid succession following their marriage in 1760 undoubtedly has something to do with the fact that the longer story in the present volume also features four daughters, whereas the standard multiplier in traditional tales featuring siblings is three. The youngest of the four, Marie-Anne, or Marion, was born in November 1764. The third, Élise, or Babiche, born in 1763, died at the age of seven; Marie-Anne lived with her maternal grandparents until 1770 but rejoined her parents at that point. Restif made no secret of the fact in his autobiographical writings—and even went out of his way to labor the point—that his wife had been unfaithful to him, and that he suspected that he might not actually be the father of one or more of his children.

The eldest of the three surviving children would have been in her early teens when Restif eventually began publishing the *contes bleus*, but his wife had taken them away to the provinces when the couple separated in 1773. It was not until 1785 that Marie-Anne returned to Paris to live with him, swiftly followed by the eldest daughter—named Agnès after her mother—who had left the husband she had married in 1781, and took refuge with her father. While Restif was actually writing and publishing his *contes bleus*, therefore, he was separated from all of his children—a circumstance surely not unconnected with the fact that the father of the four daughters featured in "The Four Beauties and the Four Beasts" is separated from them for many years, and is bitterly at odds with his wife in the meantime.

Of Restif's six *contes bleus*, "The Demicock" comes closest to being a straightforward tale of the marvelous, but it is also the most artificial in its construction. Although devoid of the kind of brutal satire that intrudes briefly into "The Four Beauties and the Four

Beasts" during Brancabanda's sojourn in the land of the red sheep, it does deliberately echo one of the transfigurative strategies employed by one of Restif's most august predecessors in the art of such adaptation, Jean de La Fontaine, whose satirical fables in verse were already established as classics of French literature. Restif's verse makes no attempt at poetic elegance, and is an artifice even within the context of the prose narrative, but it is nevertheless a careful nod in the direction of a particular species of respectability. The principal apologetic strategy adapted by both stories is, however, the one adapted by another author awarded classic status, Charles Perrault, who had argued that *contes bleus* modeled on folktales had an important role to play in a supposedly skeptical society because the marvelous could and ought to function as a "sugar coating" for moralistic apologues that were useful, and perhaps vital, in what he called the "*civilization*" [moral education] of children.

The two *contes bleus* are not the only fictional inclusions in *Le Nouvel Abeilard*; there are also four naturalistic narratives offered as "*modèles*" [models] for the attitudes with which children ought to be inculcated. The whole point of *Le Nouvel Abeilard* is, however, to attack the theories integrated by Rousseau into *Émile*, which take for granted the maverick philosopher's assertion that "civilization," in all the meanings of that word, is a bad thing, and that all education really ought to do is to preserve and bring out a supposed innate goodness that the influences of corrupt adult society can only spoil. Vehemently opposed to that way of thinking, Restif's text argues that the methodical "civilization" of children is, in fact, vitally necessary, and that if *contes bleus* are useful instruments to employ in that process, then their contemporary composition is not merely permissible but something that ought to be encouraged and esteemed.

Restif was, however all too well of the snag contained in that "if." There were plenty of skeptics around who suggested that telling children blatant untruths could only confuse them and promote superstition, and who were prepared to question not merely the moral effect of *contes bleus* but also their moral validity. For that reason, the rhetoric of all of Restif's *contes bleus* is remarkably anxious, perennially battling with the assumed suspicion that they are not what they pretend to be and cannot have the effect that they claim to have. That argument became much sharper over the course of the six tales, resulting in a spectacular narrative adjustment in the ultimate version of the tale of Prince O-Ribo/Oribeau, but its development is evident even in the transition between the relatively casual and imaginative unfettered account of "The Demicock" and the much more elaborate and distinctly uneasy account of "The Four Beauties and the Four Beasts."

From the viewpoint of a modern reader, of course, the acuity with which Restif felt the problem of justification is likely to seem a trifle exaggerated. After a further two centuries and more, we are very well aware of the fact that *contes bleus* have not died out in the course of the Age of so-called Enlightenment, but have actually gone from strength to strength, albeit in the face of constant suspicion and hostility. Many writers nowadays feel free to indulge their imagination simply for the sake of doing so, and are reasonably confident that doing so will not be an insurmountable barrier to publication and the appreciation of readers. Even so, the perceived need for apology and justification has not disappeared, and the battle against naked hostility still has to be fought, over and over again.

It is, therefore, still possible to sympathize with Restif's perceived predicament and to appreciate his ingenuity in attempting to excuse his endeavors. The two stories in the present volume only represent the first steps in that personal war, and it is in the introduction and annotations to the companion volume that its final phases will be sketched in order to provide a context for the stories themselves, but it ought to be noted here that it was a private war that Restif—or, at least, the Fée Ouroucoucou—lost. After publishing the final version of the story of Prince Oribeau, he wrote no more tales of fays. The drastic narrative adjustment that he made in that final tale killed off "the noble fay," and he subsequently exercised his extraordinarily prolific and eccentric imagination in other contexts of credulity, with the aid of different narrative means.

The six *contes bleus* that Restif did produce between 1775 or thereabouts and 1785, however, and the strategies he employed in order to get them into print in a marketing environment that he perceived, correctly, as inhospitable, remain fascinating examples of a particular phase in the evolution of fantastic fiction, and of one exceptional author's contribution to that progress. They are atypically long, partly because Restif was naturally garrulous and partly, in the case of "The Four Beauties and the Four Beasts," because of the intensive recomplication of its standard motif. The author probably planned to publish the latter as an independent volume, but either failed to find a publisher or abandoned the project of his own accord; either way, it is an interesting early contribution to what is by now a rich tradition of *contes bleus* that approach novel length rather than being carefully confined to the dimension of a short story. Like all pioneering exercises, it is a trifle tentative in venturing into trackless literary territory, but it certainly has no lack of enterprise.

The following translations were made from the copies of volumes two and three of *Le Nouvel Abeilard* reproduced on Google Books, although it was necessary to refer to the Slatkine facsimile editions reproduced on *gallica* to fill in the text on one page that is cut in half vertically in the Google scan. The translation was complicated by the fact that Restif, who typeset all his own books, had certain eccentricities unique to him, including idiosyncratic modifications of spelling and, most frustratingly, the fact that he used an identical symbol for the lower case letter f and the long s. Although it is usually possible to work out from context whether, for instance, "Je fais" is supposed to mean "I do" or "I know," it is not always clear how the symbol is to be translated in invented proper names, or in the anagrams of which the author was fond. The consequent problems are probably not unconnected with the fact that neither *Le Nouvel Abeilard* nor *Les Veillées du Marais* has ever been reprinted in France, except in Slatkine's photographically-reproduced facsimile editions, and in recent scanned versions.

Brian Stableford

THE DEMICOCK

Once, in ancient times, in Étivé in Burgundy, there was a man named Songecreux, who was very knowledgeable, for he could read in the stars as if in a book, and he made verses as good and fine as Nostradamus has made since; it has even been claimed that Nostradamus stole his prophecies from him. He was an astrologer and a poet, so he was poor, so poor that he did not have a sou.

No longer knowing what to do in order to live, he became a reviewer of authors. That wretched métier was even more disastrous for him than the other two. One evening, when he was coming back a little late to the city of Sirap, he was attacked by two authors, named Bouhcricracrah and Tututlititi, about whom he had not spoken well—for his poverty was the cause of his always being in an ill humor—who hit him with sticks so many times that he was left for dead. That made him renounce forever the métier of reviewer of authors; but he might just as well have continued, for he fell ill of malnutrition.

Ready to yield up his soul, Songecreux summoned his two sons, whom he had had during his marriage to the daughter of an alchemist, who had passed all his wealth through the crucible searching for the philosopher's stone.

"Oh, my children," he said to them. "I'm going to die of an incurable malady—I can assure you of that, because it's hunger. I fear that you it will soon harvest you as well. We're living in a century in which everyone desires science but no one encourages it. I therefore encourage you, Chatbourré, my elder, to give up astrology, in spite of your rare progress in that illustrious art, and you, Melimelo, my younger, poetry, at which you excel. Rather become, you Chatbourré, who are strong, a street-porter, and you, Melimelo, who are more delicate, a ladies' hairdresser; those métiers are not noble, but at least they nourish their masters."

"No," replied the elder, brutally. "I want to be a monk, or a physician, or a reviewer of authors."

"The first of those métiers," replied the dying man, "nourishes its master without him doing anything, whereas in mine I have worked hard without being nourished; in the second, bad work is better recompensed than good; but in the third, there is nothing to be earned but beatings. Better to be a street-porter."

"I'm strong, and I shall give as good as I get," replied Chatbourré.

"As for me, Papa," said Melimelo, "I'll do whatever I can, except for poetry, since you forbid me that."

"My children," the dying man went on, "if you want to avoid my sad end, don't make poems and don't read the stars; as for beatings, you're free to try them out if your heart bids you to do so. My father-in-law, your grandfather, the clear-sighted Soufflisoufflinsoufflot, the father of your good mother, the lame Dicidela, who died of a suffocation of speech, had a science much better than mine; he might have made gold if he had only lived to be a hundred, but he died at ninety-nine years and eleven months, on the very eve of transmutation. He told me so as he expired, like me, for lack of soup.

"However, he had not wasted his time completely; while making his alchemical experiments he had found something he wasn't looking for: the secret of making a cock live forever by dividing it in two, in such a fashion that of each of its double members, each half had one, and the others were split down the middle. He had in his poultry-yard a cock that had undergone several experiments, such as having its head cut off and stuck back on, its intestines removed and replaced and a thousand other things—what do I know?—and everything was instantly repaired, unless a man full of all the vices had eaten the amputated part, for then it was necessary to wait twenty-four hours to cur from that wretch as much flesh as he had eaten of the immortal cock, which would then replace the devoured limb.

"Alas, though, that very beautiful discovery completed the alchemist's misfortune. The cock being immortal, only able to be eaten in conditions worse than his distress, he was unable to make a soup of it to prolong his life until the conclusion of his great wok. He died...

"As your poor late mother, the lame Dicidela, was the great Soufflisoufflinsoufflot's only daughter, I had the cock for an entire heritage. I did nothing with it, not knowing what purpose immortal cocks might serve, except to let their masters die of starvation. Your grandfather had told me, however, that it might be a great help to me—but what confidence can one have in a man who is dying of hunger?

"I think, personally, and I tell you so with confusion, that a man who dies of hunger is more dishonored than a man who is hanged. So, I still have the cock—look, there it is, putting its head under the door. I locked it in that cupboard, where it has eaten whatever it could, for that which can't nourish anyone is unworthy of being nourished...

"That's your entire legacy, my sons. As for my astrological instruments...three days ago...I smashed them...no one having wanted them...for an obol... Adieu...I sense...a fallib..."

Songecreux was unable to finish the word. He had taken on one so big that it was his last. His two sons buried him themselves, for want of anything with which to pay a gravedigger, and then came back to divide their inheritance, which consisted of the dead man's straw mattress, which it was necessary to burn, and the immortal cock.

The two brothers were in great embarrassment. If the mattress had been any good, one of them could have had the mattress and the other the cock, but there was only the cock. They went to see it.

"Oh, how scrawny it is," said Chatbourré. "It's only good for boiling; if you want, we could make soup with it."

"You know what my father said."

"Right! He was rambling," said Chatbourré—for he was not very respectful. "I don't believe that nonsense, told to us by an old man whose head was as empty as his stomach. Then again, I like to tear things apart."

"You'll do well as a journalist, then," said Melimelo. "Personally, I don't want to eat that poor cock. I wouldn't be much further forward when I'd eaten half a scrawny cock. Let's draw lots instead, to determine who has it."

"No," said Chatbourré. "I'm not as lucky as you, and I can't risk having nothing at all for a heritage, as in the paternal heart. We have to share. I'd rather nourish myself than nourish it; I only live for myself."

"Oh, very good—you're going to be a monk, then?"

"I'll be whatever I want. Come on, grab the cock."

"But how are we going to divide it?"

"Down the middle, cutting it in such a fashion that each half has one eye, one wing and one leg."

"Will you have the heart to martyrize the poor beast like that?"

"Oh, I'm not so soft-hearted, me, and I'd cleave a man in two who'd be of some use to me, just like that rooster."

The younger brother started to weep, saying: "You'd do better, then, to become a physician," while the elder sharpened his knife on a shard of an earthenware pot, the sad debris of the parental succession.

Then, Chatbourré having taken the cock, which was very tough, Melimelo said: "I'll give you the whole cock."

"If I wanted it, I wouldn't need your consent! It's necessary to split it."

As Chatbourré picked up the knife, however, a plaintive voice said: "The brother...who is dividing...the cock...is wicked. He shall only have a dead half...all the life will pass...into his brother's."

"Do you hear that?" said Melimelo, frightened.

"That's what I want—I'll eat my half," Chatbourré replied, laughing. "It'll be split in two..."

At the same time, Chatbourré took the cock by the feet and *snap!* he split it in two like a turnip.

He kept one half, and threw the other to his brother, scornfully, saying to him: "Here, simpleton, that's your share."

But his brother's half immediately started walking, hopping on one foot, while his own remained dead, without even twitching, as chickens do when their heads are cut off.

Chatbourré was quite content, and mocked Melimelo, saying to him: "You alone have the immortal cock, which is good for nothing. As for me, I'm going to eat my part, but you'll only get the foot and the half-beak. And he went to have his half cooked in the home of a lady of his acquaintance named Faribolifaribola, who only received those who brought her something. The meal wasn't huge, but those women seize everything with both hands, saying that "little streams make great rivers."

As for Melimelo, he would rather have died of hunger than touch his demirooster, even if he could have killed it. He put it on a dung-heap in order that it could search there for subsistence, and as soon as the demicock had rolled in the dirt everything was consolidated; in less than an hour, it recovered plumage, which covered the new skin, but it still only had one eye, one wing, one foot and half of its whole body.

When it was fully healed, it started scratching the ground in search of its nourishment, and every day, when Melimelo came home from work, as his father had recommended him to do in order to earn a living, his half-puller ran toward him singing a long cock-a-doodle-doo. Then it went back to its dung-heap, as if it wanted to tell him to follow it. At first, Melimelo did not pay any great attention to that, but in the end, seeing that it happened every day, he mentioned it to his brother.

It is necessary to know that Chatbourré, instead of becoming a street-porter, as his father had advised, had become a physician, on the advice of Faribolifaribola, a salamander of the Sirap Arepo[1]—for he liked that méti-

---

[1] The use of salamanders (fire elementals) as temptresses was not commonplace in eighteenth-century French literature, but

er, in order to make poor people suffer more easily without anyone being able to complain about it. He had gone to work for an old doctor named Rebarbatin Bourelho, who had an old she-ape for a wife whom Chatbourré had pleased, to such an extent that she gave him money for his studies. So he studied, to begin with, for he had a good deal of malevolent intelligence; but with his evil dispositions and his scorn for father and mother, he did not take long to become libertine and debauched, frequenting Faribolifaribola and her daughter Falbalatine, a dancer at the Arepo.

When he had his baccalaureate he sustained three theses, in the last of which he proved that "The physician ought to follow the malady and never prevent it"—which attracted many eulogies on the part of the Faculty. It was even said that the beautiful thesis was sent everywhere in the world where there are physicians, and it became the rule there. It was on that occasion that the physicians changed Chatbourré's name to that of Chatfourré, which suited him much better. And they said to him: "We're giving you the power kill and massacre throughout society"—which gave the rascal so much pleasure that he jumped for joy.

Chatfourré, therefore, who was very knowledgeable, having heard what his brother Melimelo told him about the demirooster that sang in the evening, responded gravely, like a man familiar with nature: "Don't you see, imbecile, that it's an evil creature, which brought misfortune to our grandfather Soufflisoufflinsoufflot, the crackpot, to our father Songecreux, the simpleton, to our

---

by no means unknown; the most notable previous example was probably Thomas l'Affichard's *La Salmandre, nouvelle allegori-comique* (1744).

mother Dicidela, the gossip, and will only bring misfortune to you, more stupid than all three put together. For know that there's nothing that brings misfortune like a cock that crows in the evening So bring it to me, if it can't die, and I'll put it in a safe place."

"It will do what it can," said Melimelo, "but I'll keep my demirooster."

Chatfourré, who, by virtue of his great science, was beginning to suspect that the demicock might be very useful, wanted to have it, and he would have taken it by force if the demirooster, which had heard the dispute, had not gone to hide, so well that it could not be found. Chatfourré called "Here, chickie! Here chickie!" repeatedly, but it did not appear.

The next day, Melimelo had no work to do, because two of his best customers had abandoned him because of the nasty rumors they had heard about Faribolifaribola and Falbalatine, friends of his brother. He came back home very sad, thinking that perhaps it was his demirooster that had brought him bad luck, and he started to wonder whether he ought to give it to his brother. However, he was reluctant to do that, suspecting that if his brother had an immortal cock he would carry out experiments, to see how much a living being could suffer and how chicken liver could be swollen, making them die of listlessness, as it is said that the gourmands of Agrigento in Sicily do. For, since Chatfourré been obtaining money from the physician's wife, he regaled his mistress Falbalatine and the salamander Faribolifaribola every day.

While Melimelo was thinking about all that, however, the poor demirooster started its cock-a-doodle-doo, and, coming down from its hiding-place it came toward its master, flapping its wing as a sign of joy. That touched Melimelo's heart so much that he said, aloud: "No, even if it brings me bad luck, I won't give that poor mutilated creature away; my brother would martyrize it."

The demirooster, which heard those words—for the alchemist Soufflisoufflinsoufflot had rendered it capable of hearing and understanding our language—started scratching the ground in the courtyard, and when it had scratched hard with its foot and its half-beak, it started to sing another loud cock-a-doodle-doo and did what cocks do when they call the hens.

"How silly you are!" Melimelo said to it. "Don't you see that I have no hens here? There isn't enough to eat for you; swallow, swallow; you've fasted long enough."

But the demicock still continued, looking at its master—to such an extent that, Melimelo having come closer, he saw that it was a silver coin, as big as a six-livre piece, that his demirooster had just found, and was showing him. The young man picked it up, saying: "My demirooster's already found me more than it's worth, enough to make several stews like my brother's." And he was so pleased that he went to fetch a handful of barley, which he gave to the demirooster.

Afterwards, he examined the coin, and saw that it was not local currency. He was annoyed. He went to sell it to a scholar who had been a friend of his father, thinking that at least he would get the weight. But he found that it was a beautiful antique medallion, very rare, for which he was given a purse full of gold, which was less than half its value.

As soon as Melimelo had that purse, he bought a little house to live in, with a yard and a garden, and he made a very nice chicken-run for his demicock. Afterwards he resumed work, for fear of losing the habit, and also to try to amass some savings, in order to marry some pretty girl and be happy. That had been his sole desire for a long time, and he was so gentle that all the girls liked him, whereas they had always fled Chatfourré, who was very jealous of Melimelo in consequence. But they had liked him in vain; their parents said to them: "Don't go falling in love with the astrologer Songecreux's son; he's a good-for-nothing who'll die of hunger like his father."

As soon as he had bought his house, though, everyone began to be polite to him, and said: "How was he able to buy that house, a hairdresser?"

"It just goes to show," old women said, "that vanity goes a long way these days; even maidservants and shopgirls are getting their hair done; if it goes on, it'll no longer be possible to recognize respectable women."

The person who was most surprised was Chatfourré. He came to see Melimelo to ask him whether he had found the secret of making gold. The younger brother relied to his elder that he had not, and told him quite simply that his demirooster, while scratching, had found a rare medallion as big as a six-livre piece, which had brought him a purse full of gold, for it was an Othon.[2]

Chatfourré was very afflicted on hearing what Melimelo told him, and he repented of having divided the rooster in order to eat his share like a glutton, but there was no longer any remedy for it. He said to his brother: "Half of it belongs to me, for we're brothers, and besides, I didn't get my half of the immortal cock,

---

[2] The Roman Emperor Otho, who reigned briefly in 69 A.D., well-known in France as the protagonist of Pierre Corneille's tragedy *Othon* (1664).

since my half remained dead and yours lived; if mine had lived I wouldn't have eaten it."

"I want everything that you want," his brother said to him. "Half my house is yours."

"No," said Chatfourré. "I want the money." That was in order to spend with the salamander Faribolifaribola and the dancer Falbalatine, her daughter.

"Wait until tomorrow," said Melimelo, meekly, "and I'll sell half my house to give you your share."

"Don't fail to do it!" said Chatfourré, going away angrily.

That same day, Melimelo went to see an old miser named Lamauvaisannée, who had a great deal of money and lived three leagues away in a village called Iranci.

"Monsieur," he said, "I've heard that you have a great deal of money and I've come to sell you half my house in Étivé, because my brother Chatfourré, the physician, says that half of it is his and he wants to have it in money."

"I don't have any, my child," said the old miser, coughing, *ahem, ahem.* "they're evil tongues who've told you that…but if you want to make a good deal on the whole house, I'll go find an old woman who lives three leagues away in Coulanges, who'll lend it to me, *ahem, ahem.*"

I need it today."

"How much, *ahem, ahem?*"

"Three hundred écus, the half," said Melimelo.

"I'll give you a hundred and fifty for the lot, and everything here is in the house, above it and below, for a hundred thousand feet underground, and a hundred feet up in the air will be mine, for as one makes one's bed, one must lie in it, *ahem, ahem.*"

Melimelo argued a little, but he couldn't get anything better than selling the whole house for three hundred écus, which was the sum he had to give Chatfourré. The miser paid him after the contract was signed; Lamauvaisannée only had the generosity of allowing the young man until the following day to find somewhere else to live.

So Melimelo came back from Iranci with his money, very sad, and went to find his brother that same evening. He said to him: "Here's your share of the money I got for the medallion, but I no longer have the house, because old Lamauvaisannée only gave me half of what it cost me."

"That's all right," said Chatfourré. Your demicock will find another, and you'll give me my half before buying anything. But since Lamauvaisannée only paid half, we'll see..."

And as soon as Chatfourré had his brother's money he thought that it would never end. He went to buy himself fine clothes, and set about having a good time with the salamander Faribolifaribola and the dancer Falbalatine, while Melimelo, very weary and very sad, went to bed, very anxious about where he would lodge the following day.

He scarcely slept all night and got up at the first crow of the demicock, thinking about what he had to do, because he had to move out of the house very quickly in order to leave it to Lamauvaisannée. As he opened his bedroom door, however, he heard someone knocking on the door to the courtyard.

"Who's there?"

"A friend."

"Is that you already, Monsieur Lamauvaisannée?"

"No, no, open the door."

"Who are you, then?"

"I'm Mère Lépargne, who's come to talk to you."

He opened the door. It was a woman about fifty years old, but still sprightly and sturdy, who said to him, frankly: "I've come to see you, my dear Melimelo, because I have a daughter as beautiful as the day and as clever as the fays, and I've come to offer her to you in marriage, with a good dowry. You brother asked me for her, but he's too nasty and I don't like him at all; anyway, he spends every day with Faribolifaribola and Falbalatine.

"The frippery-merchant whose daughter cuts capers at the Arepo?"

"Yes, a merchant! She's really a salamander who's disguised herself thus on the advice of the Great Lustucru, liege-lord of the gnomes of the Black Forest, her lover. Chatfourré loves young Falbalatine, and he's their physician. But to get back to our business, your house is very nice, it pleases me as much as you please my daughter; we'll come and live here with you."

"Alas, Madame," said Melimelo, "my poor house was sold yesterday."

"What! You, who I thought so sensible, have sold your property?"

"Alas, Madame, it was to give my brother his half of the medal my demirooster found."

"Explain that to me."

He explained everything to her, and the good woman shook her head, saying: "In that case, adieu. When you have something, we'll see." And she went away.

Melimelo was very sad, for he had heard mention of the woman's daughter, who was rich, pretty and of good character. He said to himself: "How unfortunate I am! But it was necessary to give my brother his half."

And he went to see what he could do about moving house—but it was not as difficult as he thought it would me.

He had no sooner gone out than, at ten o'clock, his brother came to the house, not to console him but to try to get his demirooster and take it away, in order to profit alone from what it found by scratching the ground. He was very content when he found that his brother was not there—not that he feared him, but he said to himself: *I'll tell him that it wasn't me who took it; I'll scold my brother for being unable to keep it, and if he earns anything, as he's hard-working, I'll still demand my half of it, to compensate me because he lost our demicock...*

As he thought that, he saw the demicock on a dung-heap, which was searching and scratching, while singing loud cock-a-doodle-doos. He crept up on it and saw that it was a large pot full of beautiful gold coins that the demicock had uncovered. He bent down very swiftly to pick it up, but the demirooster hurled itself at his eyes and would have blinded him with pecks of its half-beak if he had not let go.

"Damned demicock," Chatfourré said, "If you weren't immortal I'd already have wrung your neck..."

While he was there, in great embarrassment, and talking to himself, old Lamauvaisannée arrived on his scrawny donkey.

"There's my house! My word, it's very pretty...there's the Sun directly overhead! If it's within a hundred thousand feet, under the terms of my contract, it belongs to me, and I'll sell the daylight to everyone! What a sum per day!"

He said that aloud, not seeing Chatfourré—but the physician, who heard him, burst out laughing. Looking at him, and mocking him, he said: "And if Hell is less than a hundred thousand feet below, that's yours too, you old skinflint. But it can't escape you; you'll be taken there one day. What a sum, if you only got two liards a day from all your fellows who've gone to dwell there!"

"You said it!" replied Lamauvaiseanée, jumping for joy. "What a sum at only two liards per head..." For the villain had only retained those few words, out of a speech that had annoyed him to begin with.

"You can keep Hell and I'll keep my house," said Chatfourré, "because if you even put on a semblance of trying to take possession of it, I'll cleave you in two, as I split that demirooster you see there."

Lamauvaisannée started trembling all over on seeing the demicock and the terrible gaze that Chatfourré was darting at him.

"Monsieur," he said, "by your furry robe and your red cap I see that you're a physician; might you be, by any chance, the terrible, great and young physician who has found such a fine way of curing without remedies?"

"Yes."

"*Uh-uh-uh!*" said Lamauvaisannée, trembling at the rude tone in which Chatfourré had replied "I've heard tell, Monsieur, that when you go into your patients' homes you give them such a great fright that when you go to take their pulse, they're no longer found in bed but underneath, where they're hiding, and from which they're taken out either dead or cured, which spares them from the malady and the expense."

"Yes."

"*Uh-uh-uh!* But Monsieur, I've paid for the house."

"You've paid half. Pay me the other half, quickly, or you'll be split in two."

"Monsieur? If you split me in two, will my two halves go on living?"

31

"No, only one of them, like that cock."

"Who'll only eat half as much?"

"Yes."

"Who'll only need half a coat, one shoe, one stocking, one trouser-leg, one glove, half a short and half a hat?"

"Yes, yes."

"Oh, Monsieur, split me, I beg you."

"Yes, I'll do you that favor if you pay me the other half of the price of the house."

He was, I believe, about to cleave him in two, and the miser was about to lend himself to it, in order to save twice as much, when old Lamauvaisannée perceived the pot of gold discovered by the demirooster. At that sight, all his senses were suspended momentarily, but he soon recovered twice as much vigor as he had ever had before and launched himself upon the treasure. The demicock was not asleep, and lacerated him with pecks of its half-beak, but the miser, bloodied, did not want to let go.

"It's mine, damned demicock!" he cried "unless you can prove that you found it more than a hundred thousand feet deep. Now…it's easy to see…that's not…"

A peck of the half-beak in the only good eye that Lamauvaisannée still had prevented him from seeing anything.

"I can no longer see, but I take you as a witness, Monsieur," he shouted at Chatfourré—who was laughing with all his might and coming forward to take advantage of the dispute by carrying off the pot of gold—"that the pot was only half a foot deep…"

But Chatfourré was not there yet. The miser was holding on to the pot of gold, the demicock was holding on to the miser, and he would have had to drag away the pot, the miser and the demicock.

Chatfourré was about to get rid of the miser by cutting off his hands when a horseman dressed in red went
past the house, as tall as a perch and as stiff as a cuckoo,
who, having seen the pot of gold, descended from his
mare in order to come and get it. Chatfourré tried to bar
his way, but the tall stiff man gave him a flick that sent
him to fall twenty paces away, even though he was very
robust, took the pot by the handle and lifted it up like a
feather along with the miser, who was determined not to
let go, and was still saying: "I take you all as witnesses
that it was less than a hundred thousand feet underground..."

The tall man dressed in red put everything on his
mare, in spite of the representations made to him, in
gnomish language, by the demicock, and drew away at a
trot, making the miser bounce on the horse's rump like a
rabbit-skin, while the demicock followed, hooping along
and shouting and cock-a-doodle-dooing:

"Stop, Lustucru!
"Give me back my due!"[3]

The one who was left behind, stunned, was
Chatfourré, but he consoled himself, thinking that he
only had to appropriate the house. First he took the miser's donkey and took it home. Then he went to find his
brother and told him that he had been to see him, in or-

---

[3] Because the rhyming of the couplets is vitally important to
the story I have had to improvise considerably in order to replace them in the translation; the lines in question are pure
doggerel even in the original, so the inelegance of many of the
improvisations is not out of keeping with the spirit of the exercise.

der to give him some good advice; how he had seen a pot full of gold coins that their demirooster had found; how the miser had come; how he had fought with the demicock; how a horseman dressed in red as tall as a perch and as stiff as a cuckoo, who could send people flying twenty paces with a flick, had come and lifted up the pot and the miser like a feather; how his demicock had talked gnomish better than Cicero; how it had not been heeded any more than a clergyman preaching temperance to drunkards; and how the horseman had ridden away at a trot, while the demicock hopped after him cock-a-doodle-dooing:

"Stop, Lustucru!
"Give me back my due!"

Having heard all that, Melomelo returned home, and, having found that his demicock was no longer there, he began to weep, saying: "Demirooster, Demirooster, where are you? What has become of you, Demirooster? Shall I never hear your cock-a-doodle-doos again, then? Alas! Alas!"

He started lamenting, and he lamented for two days, in the morning, before going to work, and in the evening, when he came home—for he had not changed lodgings, seeing that Lamauvaisannée had not come back. However, his brother, who was burning to take possession of the pretty house, but did not dare not throw him out overtly because of what people would say, wove an evil scheme against Melimelo with Faribolifaribola—which, however, did him no good.

On the third evening, as Melimelo was lamenting, as usual, he heard a loud noise, like a young woman's screams. The young man, who was good and kind, got up and ran to help. In the darkness he glimpsed three thieves who were dragging way a girl as beautiful as the day, in order to put her in a cart. The young woman was weeping and saying: "No, I don't want to go with you to your cavern, where you'll do with me what you did with my poor maidservant Recurette, who is perhaps being eaten by the gnomes at this moment!"

Melimelo sensed all his blood congealing at these words, but soon, gathering is courage, he started shouting: "Hola! Hey, George, Bastien, Jérôme, Gilles, Antoine, Paphnuce, Guillaume, Matthieu, Charlot, Thomas, call all your comrades and come here with your knives, your axes, your sickles and your pitchforks, to cut, slash and smash these villainous thieves, who want to take this nice young woman to their cavern!"

The thieves, hearing that, thought they had an entire village on their heels; they were so frightened that they let go of the young woman and ran away.

Melimelo was all the more pleased to have rescued the young woman because she was very pretty. He untied her, because her hands were bound behind her back, and then said to her respectfully: "Beauty, I'm yours. Where would you like me to take you?"

"Alas, the thieves might have killed my good mother, after having robbed her, and there's no one at home."

"Beauty, if you'll permit it, I'll take you to my house, and you'll be the mistress there."

"Alas, I dare not, for my mother had amassed a good dowry in order to marry me to a virtuous young man, who has sold his house in order to give the money to his brother, and my mother said to me: 'Boutonderose, never look a man in the eyes if he isn't the husband you ought to have; he isn't rich but he has something worth more than riches, generosity. Your dowry is good, but virtue is worth more...' The thieves have stolen my dowry; I have nothing left but virtue."

"O Beauty, what is this young man's name?"

"Melimelo."

"He's the man you see, who would rather die a thousand times than assault your virtue."

Boutonderose blushed like a rose in bloom and allowed herself to be taken to Melimelo's house.

When she had recovered somewhat from the fright that the thieves had given her, the young man asked her to tell him how she and her good mother had fallen into their hands, and whether there was any means of liberating Mère Lépargne.

"Alas," said Boutonderose, weeping, "the person who caused us this misfortune is a certain Chatfourré, a physician, who asked my mother for me in marriage, but she refused him as a son-in-law because he's a bad lot, who treats the sick brutally when they're poor, and yields to all their caprices when they're rich, without troubling himself with curing them."

"That's my brother," said Melimelo, "and I don't recognize him in that description; you must be mistaken."

"Oh, no, for he's the friend of the salamander Faribolifaribola, who, having spent everything on frippery, wants to have the wealth of others; and she's the one who wanted to kill my mother and who made...made...poor Recurette, our maidservant...in spite of the fact that she begged Faribolifaribola for mercy, who mocked her, while Chatfourré extracted her teeth, in order to give them to the old salamander, who has a daughter named Falbalatine, who...who...who..." She dared not finish.

Melimelo was about to respond in order to excuse his brother when they heard a horse whinny. "There they are, coming back," said Boutonderose, trembling.

"Let me go and see," said Melimelo; and he went to listen at a little door to his garden—but he could not hear anyone, so he approached gradually, on tiptoe, the place where the horse had whinnied, and found that the thieves had left their bay horse and their covered cart. He took the horse by the bridle and brought the cart into the courtyard; then he put the horse in the stable.

"What was it, then?" asked the young woman, who was waiting for him, trembling all over. "Beauty, it's their bay horse and their covered cart, which the thieves left behind."

"Uncover the cart, young man, and look inside."

Melimelo uncovered the cart and looked inside. He found that there were four sacks full of silver, which would have been worth a hundred thousand francs in today's money, for he counted it in front of the Beauty, who said to him: Alas, young man, that's my dowry, but who will return my mother to me?"

"Beauty, I'll go put the dowry in our room, and when my misfortune dictates that you leave me, you'll take it with you."

"No, that money is yours," said Boutonderose, blushing. "It was stolen; it was lost; you've found it; it's yours."

"Beauty, if I kept it I'd resemble the thieves who it from you. No, no; instead of taking your wealth, I wish I had some to offer you."

Boutonderose started smiling, which surprised Melimelo a great deal. "Thank you," she said to him, "but your refusal hurts me, for I'll always be in your debt for the service you've rendered me, unless..."

"It's me, Beauty, who will be in your debt for the honor that you're doing me today. And may it please God that I'll be able to find Madame Lépargne, your honorable mother! I'll go to search for her this evening. As for riches, if I hadn't had the loss that I suffered three days ago, perhaps I'd have as much."

"What have you lost, then?" Boutonderose asked him, curiously.

"Alas, I had a demirooster that found medallions worth six hundred silver écus and pots of golden coins. But a horseman dressed in red, who can knock a man down with a flick, has taken the pot of gold; my poor demirooster ran after him, and I no longer have either the pot of gold or the demirooster."

"So it was yours, then, the demirooster that I saw hopping after a horseman who riding at a trot on a dappled gray mare?"

"Yes, Beauty, it was mine, and I weep for it every way, but your presence has dried up my tears.

"You'll soon have new ones, for there's much talk about you."

"So much the better, Beauty. But can't you finish telling me how the thieves attacked you and your good mother? For that can't have been my brother."

"Oh, young man, you're good and don't believe evil, but your brother is a wicked man, who doesn't like work, saving or virtue. He became a physician in order to abuse an estate in which one doesn't see clearly and in which there are as many knaves as fools, so my mother says. If there weren't any physicians, he'd have become a monk, and if there weren't any monks he'd have become a beggar, and if there weren't any beggars he's have become a thief, and if the law had prevented there being any thieves, he'd have become a spy, for anything

38

would have been equal for him, in order to get money. That's all I can tell you."

She showed her hands and touched her eyes and ears, which Melimelo understood. Finally, she added: "Now, go to bed and sleep; I shall also get some sleep, if you have a room where I can lock myself in."

"Oh, Beauty I have one, but you have nothing to fear from me."

"I know that, Melimelo. Who refuses the purse does not touch the honor, but every virtuous young woman wants to lock herself in, for modesty is like peach-blossom."

"Beauty, this is your room, and sleep as if you were under your mother's wing."

Boutonderose locked herself in and Melimelo went to bed; as he was very tired, he went to sleep.

He had not been in bed long, and was beginning to fall asleep when he was woken up by frightful screams. Alarmed, Melimelo leapt out of bed and ran to Boutonderose's door.

"What's the matter, Beauty?"

"Young man! Young man! Break down the door, break down the door, for I've found a tiger here that will tear me apart!"

Melimelo broke down the door, but was very surprised when, in the moonlight, he saw his older brother lying on the floor, in a pool of his own blood.

"Oh, wretch that I am! I've received a Beauty in my house who has killed my poor brother."

"Don't weep, young man," said Boutonderose. "I knew that your brother had hidden in this room, and that he was going to kill you tonight, in order to have your house, for Faribolifaribola had told him that the miser from Iranci would not come back again, because the

39

Great Lustucru, Prince of the Gnomes of the Black Forest, had drowned him while passing over the Talking River. But I could only help you on certain conditions, which have been fulfilled. There are many others, more difficult; that's all that I can tell you. As for your brother, he's asleep. Put him in the covered cart, hitch the bay horse to it and leave before daybreak, for fear of being seen.

"The bay will take you to the Black Forest, and when you've arrived in a place where the horse whinnies, while striking the ground with his hoof, get down and look in the grass for a large iron ring. Pull it with all your might until you've raised a trap-door that covers a large subterrain. The bay will go in; close it very quickly, without being frightened, without listening and without stopping, and above all without rhyming, no matter what anyone says. Go on, without looking behind you, and don't reply if anyone calls to you. Always avoid the paths to the left until you've emerged from the forest.

"Two hundred paces further on, in a path so little trodden that it's green with chives and covered in strawberries, you'll find a fox in a blue jacket, which will speak to you. You must continue on your route, and further on, you'll find a wolf in a gray cloak, which will speak to you, but you must still continue your route, until you find the Talking River."

"Oh, Beauty, you're making fun of me!"

"No. If you're faithful, the effect will prove everything I tell you, and you'll find me again in your house; but if you fail, you'll cause a great misfortune."

Melimelo picked up his brother's body, weeping, and loaded it into the cart, saying: "Alas, alas, why didn't you ask me for the house? I would have given it to you, and everything else besides."

He hitched up the bay and departed before daybreak for fear of being seen, allowing the horse to guide him as Boutonderose had said. He soon arrived at the Black Forest, and when he had walked for a long, long time the bay began to whinny and struck the ground with its hoof.

Immediately, Melimelo leapt out of the cart. He bent down and searched in the grass, where he found the large iron ring, which he started pulling with all his might, until he had raised a large trap-door that covered a subterrain.

As soon as the trap-door was open, the bay leapt into it with the cart, whinnying, but Melimelo was so frightened, on hearing more than a thousand voices in the subterrain that he could not close it again, with the consequence that terrifying fleshless specters emerged from it, which fluttered around him, saying:

"Is someone there?
"It's Récurette!"

Without thinking, Melimelo replied, rhyming in spite of himself:

"No, it's the bay mare
"And her wagonette."

As soon as he had rhymed, all the specters started screeching and flying, like house-martins when it is going to rain, and even the shade of Songecreux appeared to his afflicted son, which caused Melimelo to flee, while raucous voices said:

"It's a meal you'll get,
"From Récurette!

"Lovely girl! What a honey!
"She doesn't steal money!"

With that, Melimelo had no doubt that they were ogres, and that the Beauty he had helped had only come expressly to deceive him and kill his brother—for fear rendered him credulous. And, remembering what she had told him about the fox, the wolf and the Talking River, he thought: *How stupid I've been!*

That is why, instead of doing what Boutonderose had told him to do and avoiding all the paths to the left, he took that accursed direction, along a tortuous little path, running as fast as he could and fearing that he had all the ogres on his heels, for he could hear the people from the cavern saying: *"Chit! Chit! Oh! Oh!"* But he fled even more rapidly.

When he was far away, very far away, he found himself at dusk on the edge of the forest. He went into a great plain, on the far side of which he discovered a large château build on a hill; but as he drew nearer to it he saw that it could not be reached, because it was surrounded by water like a sea, for two leagues around.

Melimelo was very annoyed by that inconvenience, for he could not have been wearier and he was very hungry. But how could he traverse that sea without a boat? He could not see one, and he was obliged to lie down behind a bush in order to try to go to sleep, in spite of the pangs of his stomach, which did not listen to reason. He slept quite well, however, except that he had bad dreams, and he only woke up in broad daylight the next day.

When he was awake, however, and had yawned, rubbed his eyes, stood up and looked at the château, he was quite astonished no longer to see the sea, and to find all the country dry, beautiful and verdant. He was full of joy, and hastened to arrive.

When he entered the courtyard of the château he found everyone busy salting sheep, ewes and goats, of which there were more than two thousand whose throats had been cut; there were also five or six thousand hens, roosters and capons lying dead here, which the master of the château was giving at a sou apiece to anyone who wanted one. In a meadow, there were all the men, women and children from the surroundings, who had lit fires, over which they were roasting mutton and poultry for a feast, while all of it was virtually free.

Melimelo, who was extremely hungry, devoured that good cheer with his eyes. He approached a table where there seemed to be good people, and asked whether they would permit him to eat if he paid.

"Yes," said a father. "For eighteen deniers you can eat as much as you like."

"Much obliged, Monsieur; I'll sit down." And he sat down at table, where he ate like four.

When he had appeased his hunger somewhat, he started to ask questions.

"Can you tell me, Monsieur, what is the festival that's being celebrated today?"

"It's not a festival, young man, but rather a mourning; and if you wish, I'll tell what it's about while you eat, for it would be a pity to make you miss a bite."

"Oh, that would give me pleasure, Monsieur. And you can also tell me what became of the sea that was around this château yesterday."

"Yes, yes—all that's connected."

And the old man began to narrate, as follows:

Young man, who has such a fine appetite, you couldn't have chosen a better time to travel, for in any other season you'd have died of hunger here. Know that this château belongs to a very noble and very powerful lord, Monseigneur Croquetout among humans, the Great Lustucru among the gnomes of the Black Forest, whose Prince he is; Duc de Sausserobert, Comte de Lafricassée, Marquis du Rôt, Vicomte d'Andouilles, Baron de Languefourrée, Seigneur de Jambon, Risedeveaux, Piedsdemouton, Civet, Pâté, Cervelats, Boeufalamode, Haricot, Potaufeu and other places.

It's four or five days since our master, who is as tall as a perch and as stiff as a cuckoo, came back on his dappled gray mare from visiting the salamander Faribolifaribola, whose daughter he loves: young Falbalatine, a dancer at the Sirap Arepo, as red-haired as a cow, with eyes like a pig, vainer than a peacock, more coquettish than a hoopoe, and more impudent than a goat—which means that she spends a lot and has already ruined half a dozen gnomes or land-Lords. Our master, therefore, seeing that he'd need a lot of money to maintain that salamander in nice clothes, was thinking about all that with chagrin while coming back to his Château de la Blanquette here.

And while he was dreaming, he saw, or thought he saw, the specter of his father, the great Lustucuit, as nasty when he was alive as yellow blubber, and nicknamed Fessematthieu, who gave him a good slap and said to him:

"Psst! Psst! I see that you're only thinking about spending what I had so much trouble accumulating, you great good-for-nothing. You're maintaining she-apes who are making mock of you and who need new dresses every day, while your poor late mother, the good

Filinfilifila wore a calimanco skirt for twenty-five years without wearing it out, for it was only dirty and didn't have a single hole. Wretch!

"You don't deserve it, but I feel sorry for you. You see that pretty little house that belongs, without belonging to him, to the grandson of a famous alchemist to whom I lent money at high interest for as long as he had had assets in the sun, and who died of hunger so inconveniently that if he had only lived one second more he'd have discovered the universal panacea and the philosopher's stone? There's a treasure there; go and get it, but only take that and don't make a mistake; nourish it well and never let go of it."

As he finished, the old specter disappeared, clinking a few copper coins that the Devil had let him keep in order to amuse himself.

Lord Lustucru, who is a great Necromancer, understood all that quite easily, and, having perceived a demirooster, the alchemist Soufflisoufflinsoufflot's masterpiece, scratching the ground, he had no doubt that it wasn't there for plums. He got down from his dappled gray mare and right away gave a flick to a big lout in a ermine fur who got in his way, laughing in his face and saying to him: "Out of my way, I'm a gnome and everything found in the earth belongs to me." And the lout fell twenty feet away.

Then Lord Lustucru looked, and having seen the treasure in a big pot, he threw himself on it in spite of the demirooster and a thin and dried-up man named Lamauvaisannée, from Iranci, who offered to make him a gnome, a Turk, an Arab, a Saracen or anything he wanted, as long as he left him the pot of gold, taking him as a witness that the treasure hadn't been buried more than a hundred thousand feet deep. But the great

Lustucru put the pot of gold on the rump of his dapple-gray mare, along with the thin man, who didn't want to let go of it and went on his way at a trot.

No matter how fast he went, though, the demirooster hopped after him almost as fast as him, cock-a-doodle-dooing:

"Stop, Lustucru!
"I want my due!"

And Lord Croquetout, alias Lustucru, replied:

"Go on, then, run, run!
"If you can catch me,
"In the web you've spun
"I'll see you match me!"

But the demicock kept running without stopping.

And when they were far, far away, the Great Lustucru met a handsome fox that he knew, with a blue jacket.

"Handsome friend fox,
"If you see any cocks
"On this old cart-track
"You can have a snack;
"Don't be held in check,
"Just wring me its neck."

The fox made no reply, but he thought about it anyway.

And when the Great Lustucru had gone further still, much further, he met a wolf of his acquaintance wearing a gray cloak.

"Dear wolf, old chum
"If the demicock comes,
"Along this cart-route
"You can have the loot;
"Don't be held in check.
"Just wring me its neck."

The wolf looked at him askance and made no reply, but it thought about it anyway.

And when the Great Lustucru had one further, a great deal further, he encountered a river that was familiar to him.

"River so frank
"If along your bank
"The demicock comes
"If you want my thanks,
"Don't leave its crumbs."

The river, which doesn't like the Great Lustucru, because he's in love with a salamander at the Arepo, who lives in fire, made no reply, but thought about it anyway.

And as he crossed the river, Lord Croquetout, alias the Great Lustucru, who thought that Lamauvaisannée was inconveniencing his dapple-gray mare, plunged the pot of gold into the depths of the Talking River, in order to make him let go; but the more he drowned the tighter he held on, and even when he was well and truly dead his grasping hands didn't release it, which meant that the Great Lustucru brought him here, and gave him to his barber to dissect, who found a good three ounces of gold in his brain.

But the demirooster was still following the pot of gold. When it came toward the fox in the blue jacket in its turn, they came to embrace one another wing-to-paw.

"Handsome child of amour,
"Dear Reynard, bonjour,
"For you this plain
"Is a land of Cockayne."

"What are you up to?"

"Following Lustucru,
"Who's stolen my pot;
"Have you seen him or not?"

"Yes, a big man in red
"From his feet to his head."

"Right, if I'm quick
"I'll catch him in a tick."

"I'll come, if you like."

"It might be a hike,
"If it's quite a long way."

"I can walk all day.
"I've got four feet.
"You're one might be neat,
"But just watch me run;
"I'm not soon done."

"Let's go, then, friend.
"Your strength we'll expend."

So the fox went off with the demirooster, but when they'd gone a long way, the fox could do no more.

"Damn Lustucru
"With his pot of écus!
"I've had enough;
"The going's too tough,"

he said to the demirooster, who replied by laughing, in the way that cocks laugh.

"Enough! The grass is long
"You need to be strong.
"If you'd listened to me,
"You'd be home and free.
"But climb up my backside,
"And I'll give you a ride."

The fox did what his friend suggested, and the demicock continued his route, hopping along.
When they had gone a long way they met the wolf in the gray cloak. They embraced, wing-to-paw.

"Handsome child of amour,
"Darling wolf, bonjour,
"In these lovely trees
"You must be at ease."

"Where are you bound,
"On this foreign ground?"

"Chasing the gnome-lord
"Who's stolen my hoard."

"The big man in red,
"From his feet to his head?
"He's just passed his way
"After riding all day."

"Then I'd better get on,
"Or else he'll be gone."

"I'll come, if you like."

"It might be a hike,
"If it's quite a long way."

"I can walk all day.
"I've got four feet.
"You're one might be neat,
"But just watch me run;
"I'm not soon done."

"Let's go, then, friend.
"Your strength we'll expend."

So the wolf and the demirooster set off, chatting as they went, but as it was long way, the wolf got tired.

"Damn Lustucru
"With his pot of écus!
"I've had enough;
"The going's too tough,"

he said to the demirooster, who replied by laughing, in the way that cocks laugh when they're amused.

"Enough! The grass is long
"You need to be strong.
"If you'd listened to me,
"You'd be home and free.
"But climb up my backside,
"And I'll give you a ride."

The wolf did as his friend said, and stationed himself next to the fox, and they both laughed at finding themselves there. The demicock continued its route, hopping cheerfully and comfortably.

When they were a little further on, they encountered a beautiful river known as the Talking River. The demicock and the river embraced; wing-to-wave.

"Bonjour, my old dear,
"Ever flowing here!"

"Bonjour to you too.
"Hopping so true
"Along my green shore
"But why and wherefore?"

"I'm after Lustucru
"And my pot of écus.
"Have you seen him go by?"

"Yes, he caught my eye,
"As he crossed my stream
"As if in a dream,
"With a clinking pot
"At a jolly trot."
"He stole it from me,
"And now I must flee."

"I'll come, if you like."

"But it's quite a hike,
"And you can't climb a slope;
"You haven't a hope."

"Yes, it's fine if I'm low,
"You'll see how I go.
"And even in flood
"I can still be as good
"You have my word,
"My one-legged bird."

"The fox said the same,
"The wolf was as game,
"And they don't have the gout,
"But they didn't last out.
"Their eagerness died,
"And they're up my backside."

The river started to laugh, as rivers laugh when a little fresh wind ripples the surface of the water, murmuring:

"I won't need a porter,
"I won't drink your water
"I might be some use."

"Then come, but stay loose,
"And if you start to wheeze,
"You can always join these."

So the river went on in company with the demirooster, chatting as they went. But when they have traveled a long way, the river, who was very chatty, like all females got tired. It was nothing at first, but there was a small hill there, which she couldn't climb.

"Oh, my dear demicock,
"Must we cross that rock?"

The demirooster started to laugh wholeheartedly, as cocks laugh in the morning when they coo at the hens.

"So all three of you are spent!
"Once again, my friend.
"I was right all along."

"Well, you surely weren't wrong."

"Then don't waste more time,
"Up my backside you climb."

And the river tucked up all her waters, from her source to her mouth—and even, it's said, for I can't be sure, a part of the ocean, and, with all of it reduced to the form of a large eel, she wedged herself between the wolf and the fox, along with all the carp, all the pike, all the gudgeon all the small fry, and a couple of whales that she had drawn from the Baltic Sea. The fox and the wolf, who were a little cramped, and who were very thirsty, were charmed to have the river with them, they each drank a few gulps, which refreshed them. And when the demicock had all that up its backside, it continued on its way, hopping, more cheerful and sprightly than ever.

Finally, in the evening, the demicock arrived at the Château de la Blanquette, about half an hour after Lord Croquetout, alias the Great Lustucru, Prince of Gnomes, our noble master.

"Demicock, welcome to you.
"Ah, Monsieur Lustucru.
"Return my pot of gold
"If I might be so bold."

"Tonight? It's too late
"Tomorrow, if you'll wait.
"I need something to eat
"Let's sup and be replete."

They sat down at table, in order to have an early supper, like hens, and Lord Lustucru-Croquetout treated the demicock very well.

When they had eaten their fill, they talked about going to bed.

"Fine Demicock, till sleep is done,
"We'll put you in the chicken-run"

For cocks never use a bed. The demicock was therefore put in with the chickens, where it was assumed that it would perish because of its unfortunate appearance, cocks and hens having the habit of finishing off one of their fellows seen to be half-extinct. Also, as soon as it was put in the chicken-run, the cocks, the hens, and even the capons, scenting on the stranger a certain odor of fox, started attacking him with beaks, spurs and blows of their wings, so that the desolate demicock did not know

to what saint to appeal. Then he thought about its friend
the fox.

"Help, Reynard, give me aid!
"Otherwise, I'm much afraid,
"My hide will soon be tanned
"If you don't come and lend a hand."

The fox did not have to be asked twice. It emerged
in a fury, and in less than a quarter of an hour it had
massacred the hens, the cocks and the capons, and even
the chicks, without leaving a single one alive, even
though there were five or six hundred; and when it had
completed that fine expedition its went back into the
place from which it had emerged.

The following morning, when it was time to let out
the chickens, they were very astonished to see that tragedy.

"Demicock, was this slaughter you?
"No, it's to Reynard this is due."

"There isn't any time to spare
"Let's hasten to set up a snare."

But the fox was safe.

For the sake of such a small loss, Lustucru was not
yet determined to give up the pot of gold.

"Demicock, after this affray.
"It's necessary to have fun today."

"No, I must go before the day's old
"So give me back my pot of gold.

"My master, while I'm here with you,
"Has only got dry bread to chew."

But Lustucru insisted, and it was necessary to stay. They feasted as on the previous day, and in the evening, not knowing where to put the demicock to sleep, it was lodged in the sheepfold, where it was assumed that it would perish, having nowhere to roost except the trough from which the sheep ate. And it nearly did, because the sheep, scenting a certain odor of wolf, fell upon its roost; the lambs gnawed its feathers, the horned rams butted it and the ewes trampled it underfoot. It did not know where to turn, until it remembered its friend the wolf.

"Help, dear wolf, give me aid!
"Otherwise, I'm much afraid,
"My hide will soon be tanned
"If you don't come and lend a hand."

In such a case, wolves scarcely need to be asked twice, and the one the demicock had was not lazy. It emerged immediately and massacred all the rams and ewes, and even the bleating lambs; and when it had completed that masterpiece it returned whence it had come.

And the following morning, when it was time to let out the sheep and take them to the fields, the shepherd started screaming like Mélusine. Lord Lustucru same running to see what was wrong, and see the ravage.

"Demicock, was this slaughter you?
"No, it's to a wolf that this is due."

"There isn't any time to waste

"Let's set up the traps in haste."

And the traps were set up, but the wolf was safe.

In spite of the loss he had just suffered of more than two thousand sheep, Lustucru, the Prince of the Gnomes, did not want to surrender the pot of gold as yet. He needed too much money for his Falbalatine and Faribolifaribola, and he was counting on lodging the demirooster in a place from which it would not get out.

"Demicock, all the mutton's gone.
"Let's see what we can do for fun."

"No, I must go before the day's old
"So give me back my pot of gold.
"My master, while I'm here with you,
"Has only got dry bread to chew."

But Lustucru insisted so much that it was necessary to stay.

In order better to deceive him, he was feasted more delicately than the previous evening. Lord Lustucru-Croquetout thought to himself: *You'll pay me for the loss of my chickens and ewes!*—for his necromancy had not informed him of everything that the demirooster had up its backside.

When evening came, after he had supped well, and early, like chickens, Lustucru-Croquetout took the demirooster by the foot, hid its half-head under its wing and put it to sleep, as one does with chickens, singing:

"Chirpie cheep, cheep,
"Little chickie go to sleep."

And when it was soundly asleep, he had a huge oven opened, under which he had told his gnomes to fire up until it was red hot, and he threw the demicock in, saying:

"Sleep well in that bed
"And come out dead."

And he quickly shut the over door. But as soon as the demirooster felt the heat, it started shouting:

"River, I need your aid!
"Else I'm much afraid,
"My hide will soon be tanned
"If you don't come lend a hand."

As soon as he had pronounced the first word, the river was unleashed: *splash, crash, smash, hiss, sizzle, seethe, gurgle, burble, bubble.*

The carp, the gudgeon, the eels, the small fry and the whales all came out, and the oven was very rapidly cooled, which obliged the gnomes who had heated it to run back to their subterrains, where they were all drowned.

But the person who was most put out was Lord Lustucru-Croquetout. He took refuge in the tower the Château de la Blanquette. All the rest of us, in the country, not knowing where the deluge had come from, having not had any storm, climbed trees as best we could. Finally, the waters had risen so high that our bell-ringer caught a trout in his hand, while sitting astride the weathercock on our belfry, and a whale swallowed one of our bells, which weighed thirty thousand pounds, in order to aid its digestion.

Seeing that the water was reaching his tower, however, Lustucru-Croquetout, and that a shark was showing its teeth, ready to swallow him alive, started lamenting and despairing. Then his father's specter came back to give him another slap, saying to him:

"Idiot! Didn't I tell you to pay attention to what you were taking and nourish the treasure? And can one nourish a pot, you great booby? Know that a living being is worth more than all dead riches; we, the dead, know the price of life! But you, dead or alive, have never been anything but a simpleton. Return the pot of gold right away, and if you ever speak to that she-ape Falbalatine and the salamander Faribolifaribola again, I'll come back and box your ears. But peace, the Fay Ouroucoucou will set things right, for the Mistress has already given her orders..."

And the specter disappeared, leaving Lustucru quite dazed—and when he saw the water still rising he started shouting in a resounding voice:

"Friend demicock, I'm all a-quiver,
"I beg you to take back your river,
"And you have Lustucru's sworn word
"To return your pot, you wily bird."

The demicock heard that and rapidly recalled the river, saying:

"Come on, River, back to the fold;
"Lustucru's returning my pot of gold."

Immediately, you would have seen all the water returning to the demicock's backside, more rapidly than any apothecary ever administered an enema. All that remained were a few fish, which the demicock left to pay his bill.

"Oh, Monsieur Demicock
"Your pot's in stock.
"The money's all there
"But that nasty pair
"The fox and the wolf
"And the river and gulf
"Will pay in the end.
"I thought them friends.
"I was badly mistaken;
"They've saved your bacon!"

The demicock replied, gravely:

"That's a lesson to learn,
"Though a little stern,
"To treat your friends better
"And not be their debtor.
"And then, you were wrong
"Just because you were strong
"To use all your might
"To steal—that's not right.
"You put the wrong price
"On your father's advice;
"It wasn't the gold
"But me you were told
"To return to my mother
"Without any bother.
"But I can't stay and chat
"And leave my friends flat.
"I must go find my master
"Ere he suffers disaster."

Sadly, Lustucru replied to the demicock:

"Am I not a great fool?
"But it's still rather cruel
"To lose in one tour
"Hens, sheep and amour;
"And to double the pain
"The gold's gone again!"

After that, the demicock returned, at the hop, to Melimelo's house in Étivé. When he arrived at the place where the river had been, he found the people of all the surrounding villages looking for it, and all the scholars from the nearby towns trying to explain its disappearance, saying that there was a quicksilver mine there that had hollowed out the earth, and had traced an underground route for the water.

The demirooster listened to them all without saying anything, although he knew more an all of them put together, and when they least expected it, it started crowing:

"Mother River, my thanks!
"Now return to your banks!"

And immediately, the river was unleashed: *splash, crash, smash, hiss, sizzle, seethe, gurgle, burble, bubble.* The carp, the gudgeon, the sharks, the small fry and the whales all emerged. It's even said, although I'd forgotten to mention it, that there were two or three English warships and fifty American merchant ships, and a few fishing boats that also emerged, and started sailing as if nothing had happened, in order to reach the sea, where they are at present. But the funniest thing you'd have seen was the scholars, who had been on the river bed, pulling up their long coats and running for their lives. It was marvelous. They were ashamed, although there was no reason to be. Who could have guessed, unless they'd seen it, that an entire river could be hidden in a demirooster?

As for the peasants, they were overjoyed to have their river back, even though they didn't tickle fish and it sometimes flooded; they liked habitude. As for the scholars, they were so amazed that they offered the demicock a seat in the Academy, thinking, not that it had taken the river out of its backside, but that it had caused it to return from underground by means of some secret of physics—for those people want to explain everything. The peasants, however, simply accepted the thing as it was, without looking for midday at four o'clock.

The demicock replied to the gentlemen of the Academy, without rhyming—because he was almost free of the influence of the rhyming specters—that it was too great an honor and that he had something more urgent to do; that his poor master might be dying of hunger and that before anything else, it was necessary to get his pot of gold back to him.

"You're as virtuous as you are knowledgeable," an Academician told him.

"You have people that resemble me among you, then," the demicock replied, "but I don't like praise unless it's just; I know myself, and a poor demicock like me is no more made to be lauded than sat in a chair."

"Oh," said the Academician, "it's necessary to wish that you were, in order to give some of us lessons in modesty!"

"You have models for that," said the demirooster; and with that, he hopped away.

When he reached the place from which he had taken the wolf he found all the shepherds asleep beside their sheepfolds, while the dogs were going hungry and the poor sheep were wandering on arid land devoid of grass.

"Of course," said the demicock. "I need to wake those fellows up..."

"Hey in there, don't hide;
"Come out of my backside!
"In truth, without you around
"The shepherds go to ground.
"Let's go, get on your feet;
"Tonight there's lots to eat."

Immediately, the wolf emerged and threw itself upon the poor sheep, which could only bleat, while the demicock resumed its route, cock-a-doodle-dooing in a hoarse voice:

"Wolf! Wolf! Come right away!
"Else the wolf will have his day!"

That woke up the shepherds, and all the shepherdesses—but for them, and for the sheep. it was a little too late.

When the demirooster reached the place from which it had taken the fox it found the farmers already leaving all the chickens out in the open.

"Hey in there, don't hide;
"Come out of my backside!
"Farewell, I'll leave you here;

63

"Tonight you'll have good cheer."

Immediately, the fox came out and started chasing the hens, cocks and capons, which started screeching and squawking so loudly that the farmers woke up—but it was a little too late. That will teach them to be careful.

"So now, young man," the storyteller added, "you understand the reason why we're feasting here so cheaply; it's because almost all the sheep and poultry for ten leagues around have been killed, as at the château, and we're eating them for fear that they'll spoil You can see that our Lord Lustucru-Croquetout has been well punished for trying to take the pot of gold from the demicock's poor master, the grandson of the great alchemist Soufflisoufflinsoufflot, in order to give fripperies to Falbalatine and her mother, the salamander Faribolifaribola."

"But what became of the demirooster, then?"

"It's said," the other replied, "that when he arrived at his master's house, the demirooster didn't find him—and that's all we know. We're expecting news soon, for Lord Lustucru hasn't slept. He said again this morning that if he could find the demicock's master without his damned demicock, he'd have him burned alive as a sorcerer, or a sorcerer's grandson."

Having heard that, Melimelo thought: *Let's get out of here quickly, and without saying a word.* So he paid the eighteen deniers for his food and left.

When he had traveled about two leagues, he found a great river, and men who had great chains in boats, which they were attaching to moorings on either side.

"What are you doing, good people?" Melimelo asked them.

"We're chaining this river, which has played one of its tricks on us lately, and which went on the spree.

Good, Melimelo thought. *That's the river, my demicock's friend; I need to talk to it as one talks to the fays.* And, bending down to drink, he rhymed:

"Dear river, moistening this shore,
"Please tell me, I implore.
"If you know what has become
"Of your friend demicock, in sum?"

"He went off at hippety-hop,
"With a pot of gold on top,
"He'd recovered from a gnome
"That he was taking home."

"Please tell me what occurred.
"Whatever you have heard.
"Did he arrive with diligence
"At his master's residence?"

"He discovered in the place
"A young lady fair of face,
"But his master wasn't there,
"Having gone off who knows where."

"Dear river, is that all you know?"
"Yes—it's to the wolf you must go."

Melimelo started waking again, therefore, glad to have had news of his dear demicock, and when he had covered another two leagues he found a wolf in his path, so large that he was afraid of it.

"Handsome wolf, noble and dear
"From whom I have nothing to fear,
"For I see by your honest face
"That that is certainly the case..."

"What do you want with me?"

"Only to listen to my plea;
"Tell me where I can find
"My demicock, if you'll be so kind?"

"He went off hopping at a trot,
"Carrying his precious pot.
"He'd been attached by rams and sheep,
"But I soon put all of them to sleep."

"Did he arrive with diligence
"At his master's residence?"

"He discovered in the place
"A young lady fair of face,
"But his master wasn't there,
"Having gone off who knows where."

"My brother's dead, alas, I know,
"But had he really sunk so low?"

"Boutonderose gave him directions,
"But he didn't resist deflections
"So he'll be soon in a mess
"If he isn't already in distress."

"Thank you, wolf, sincerely,
"That helps, or very nearly.

"Is that everything you've heard?"
"Yes, but the fox might have a word."

And the young man continued on his way, thinking about the Beauty that he had left in his house, resolved, after what the wolf had said, to love her and marry her, if she was not an ogress, as he had thought. And he began to be very sorry that he had not followed the route that she had indicated to him, for he said to himself: *I'd already be at home with my demicock, and I'd know everything.*

While he was thinking that he covered another two leagues, and was already very tired, when he saw a beautiful fox which was making a parasol of its tail, as squirrels do.

"Handsome fox, may God protect you,
"And never let you lack you due.
"What has befallen, do you know
"A demicock running to and fro?"

"Chickens would have plucked him bare
"But I left none to spare.
"He went off hopping at a trot,
"Carrying his precious pot."

"Did he arrive with diligence
"At his master's residence?"

"He discovered in the place
"A young lady fair of face,
"But his master wasn't there,
"Having gone off who knows where."

"My brother's dead, alas, I know,
"But had he really sunk so low?"

"Boutonderose gave him directions,
"But he didn't resist deflections
"So he'll be soon in a mess
"If he isn't already in distress."

"Thank you, fox, sincerely,
"That helps, or very nearly.
"Is that everything you've heard?"

"No, and not to mince my words,
"I've seen through your little game
"Melimelo is your name.
"If you're going home this way
"You already know you've gone astray
"And that trouble awaits ahead.
"When everything is done and said."

"Will I find when I reach the house,
"My demicock and prospective spouse?"

"Aye for one, for the other nay."

"Oh, dear fox, I'm in disarray!"

"You shall have a long remorse,
"But the demirooster, in due course,
"Will try to help you see the light,
"And do his best to put things right."

Having taken his leave of the fox, Melimelo continued on his way, and did not take long to recognize the

surroundings of his dwelling. He finally arrived at his door at the hour when chickens go to sleep. It was open.

He went into the house, but there was no one there. He immediately started calling for the demicock, which emerged from the henhouse half-asleep and uttered a hoarse cock-a-doodle-doo.

"What's become of Boutonderose?"

"I cannot tell you things like those," replied the demicock, rhyming in spite of himself.

"Why? What's getting in the way?"

"I can only tell you what I may."

"Will the Beauty ever return?"

"Her whereabouts you'll have to learn."

"But where do I begin to seek?"

"Master, the chances are looking bleak
"I have to say, it's surely true,
"Mère Lépargne is annoyed with you
"And more than a little indisposed,
"For leaving the trap-door unclosed
"For anyone to get in or out.
"And great misfortune might come about.
"Faribolifaribola might,
"If she passed that way by night.
"Have mounted an expedition.
"During the intermission.
"Lépargne couldn't go to see,

"Being imprisoned, she said to me.
"Although I don't know why
"But I fear that something's gone awry
"For Boutonderose had said
"She'd be back before I went to bed,
"Or sooner, if she could go faster."

"It's necessary, dear Demicock, that you come with
me!" Melimelo exclaimed. "I'm in despair at my fault,
and in order to repair it, I'll leave no stone unturned in
the search for my Beauty and her Mother, to help them
or perish."

At that speech, the demicock sang a great cock-a-
doodle-do and flapped its wing, saying:

"You've said it, Master!
"Oh, if you hadn't gone to the left,
"Led astray and abandoned bereft,
"On a grassy path you'd have found a fox
"In a blue coat among the rocks,
"Making a parasol of its tail,
"Which would have led you without fail
"By the hand through tunnels underground
"Where quadrupeds like him abound,
"Where you'd have traveled far
"In safety, guided by a star.
"And then a wolf in a cloak of gray
"A clever fellow, come what may,
"Would have taken you along
"Speaking well and singing a song
"As on the Sirap Alepo's stage
"Where Falbalatine is all the rage.
"The wolf would then have opened a trap
"You'd have seen a river through the gap

"Where Faribolifaribola
"You could have caught, and rolled her,
"To force her to return to you,
"Everything that was Lépargne's due
"And that was no small theft,
"Nothing of Lépargne's luxury was left.
"As soon as it had all gone through,
"Debauchery would have followed too
"In Boutonderose's regard;
"You would all have been pressed hard.
"Reynard would have burrowed,
"While the wolf made inroads,
"And Dame River flooded the redoubt,
"While you got your mistress out."

"My demicock, can't you talk to me in prose. I have a great repugnance for rhymes since my father, who died of hunger, forbade me to make them; and I have a great regret for having rhymed, out of politeness in speaking to your friends."

"Yes, Master, that will inconvenience me less, and you'll understand me better. And if it's necessary to tell you the truth, it was the two rhymes you made in the Black Forest when you returned the bay and the covered cart, that revealed the specters of all the poets who died of hunger, especially the shade of your father."

"Oh," said Melimelo. "I beg your pardon; but I didn't disobey deliberately.

"It's all right, Master; One rhymes in that place in spite of oneself."

"But why is my father there?"

"I'll explain it to you. The Black Forest is the Elysium of Poets; it's there that they all go after they die, to sigh for their imaginary Iris; but by a bizarre disposition of poetic Destiny, when poets have become chimeras, the chimerical Irises become real; they're all the actresses at the Arepo de Sirap, to which they're sent, and where they continue to be treated as princesses; but all those poet shades have a horror of rhyme, which was their torment during life, and which they could never, in spite of all their efforts, marry with reason; however, because they don't look for the accursed rhyme, it comes to them in spite of themselves, with the result that they have more pain chasing it when dead than they had finding it while alive. But let's get back to our enterprise.

"Yes, tell me what I have to do," said Melimelo, sighing.

"Come, Master; I'll take you there; and by means of a few gnomes that Faribolifaribola whose sight hasn't yet fascinated by means of Falbalatine, as well as the aid of two happy jealous lowers, if we can find them, I'll try to discover Mère Lépargne. Those good gnomes are small in number, for we're in a century where only salamanders and their nonsense are esteemed; but it's sufficient for one of us to find out, and as soon as we know where Boutonderose's mother is, the rest will follow naturally, for everything will depend on you.

"How is that, my dear Demicock?"

"As soon as we're at liberty with Mère Lépargne, you show her the pot of gold that I recovered from Lustucru-Croquetout, and she likes thrift so much that she'll forgive you for having rhymed by mistake and having forgotten to close the trap-door. And if she says to you: 'Where did you find so much money, my son?' you reply 'It's my demicock, Madame.' And if she asks for me you hand me over right away, saying: 'Even if it were a whole cock, Madame, I'd give it to you just the same.'"

Melimelo resolved to do everything that the demicock advised. He ate a piece of moldy bread that he had left before his departure, gave the crumbs to his demirooster, and then set forth with it, even though he was very tired and there was scarcely an hour of sunlight left. On the way he dreamed about Boutonderose, and how he would make her forget his errors, sighing with regret and amour.

When he and the demicock came to a beautiful meadow sprinkled with flowers, he heard the voice of a young shepherd singing:

Amour is mighty and sweet
It triumphs over the firmest courage;
You alone, rebel and savage,
Resist its assaults.

You are insensible
To all the sweetest lures;
What pleasure do you find
In our inflexible rigor.
Which will cause my death?

Imitate the young beauty
Of which an evil destiny now disposes;
But the beautiful Boutonderose,
Had not merited it.

She is tender and faithful
To the most cowardly of ingrates!
Oh, cruel man, in what a predicament
You have put that beauty
By not obeying her!

At these words, which he made out so clearly, Melimelo ran to push aside the willow branches that hid the shepherd, but he was stopped by a very soft voice, which replied:

Why trouble this peaceful place
With your clamors
About my rigors?
If favors
Are harmful
To are ardors.
In spite of your tears
Ant your languors,
I want to be inflexible;
It's over these flowers,
Where I'm dying,
That of the errors
Of young hearts
I've made the painful confession.
Your flattering eyes
Tender suborners
Are my conquerors;
No more dolors!
To your sweet talk
I am sensible.

When the voice had finished. Melimelo pushed aside the foliage, but he only saw a little wizened of man taking the fresh air and a little old woman some distance away on the grass, embroidering a beautiful flower.

"Can you tell me where the young shepherd is who was just singing, Monsieur?"

"That was me," replied the old man, in reedy voice.

Melimelo could not help laughing, but the desire he had for news of Boutonderose and Mère Lépargne made him recover his seriousness as best he could.

The wizened old man looked at him askance. "Go away," he said, "and don't look at my beauty."

"Handsome shepherd," said Melimelo, "for I don't doubt that you're enchanted; I'm asking for news of Boutonderose."

At those words the little old woman quit her flower. "Boutonderose!" she said to the wrinkled old man—for, as she was some distance away and very absorbed in her needlework, she thought it was him who had just spoken. "You're not thinking about her! But I'll imitate you, traitor!"

"Adorable jealousy, which makes me happy!" exclaimed the old man, delightedly. "Beautiful Cheveuxdorés," he said to the old woman, "I adore you uniquely. Oh, what stronger proof do you want than the plea I made to the fay Ouroucoucou to make us both old, in order not to cause us mutual jealousy. You're sixteen and I'm twenty; in you, everything is gold, lilies and roses, but you appear to other eyes than mine as a little old woman."

"You're the most handsome of shepherds," said the little old woman, languidly, "but you appear to all other eyes than mine as a wizened old man. Be tranquil; we shall love one another always. But reply to this stranger and send him away.

"Go on, Melimelo," said the young-old man, "be as constant as me if you can. You've just seen the miracle of love and beauty, but in finding Boutonderose, if you have that good fortune, you'll have the portrait of the beautiful Cheveuxdorés...oh, what do I see there? Is it Demirooster?"

"Yes, it is."

"Come here, so that I can embrace you. My name is Fleurdesoucis.

"Fleurdesoucis! Oh, what joy!"

"But you're trembling. In spite of my delicate tenderness, I shall ask Cheveuxdorés to warm you up in her bosom."

"Yes, that would calm me."

Fleurdesoucis did as he had said, although he was very jealous. Then he addressed Melimelo, saying: "When you and your Demicock reach the far side of the meadow, you'll find a mountain, which you should climb. I can't tell you any more. Adieu. Leave us..."

Melimelo left the young-old man and the young-old woman, whom their jealousy made them happy, in order to continue on his way.

When he and the demicock reached the far end of the meadow, they found the mountain that the young-old man had indicated. They climbed it. When they were at the summit, they encountered two gnomes, one an enemy and the other a friend of Mère Lépargne, of whom the demicock request news.

The first, who was young, a poet and mad, responded, sniggering:

"If the jealous young old man had seen,
"The peerless beauty receive between
"The apples of her lovely breasts
"The cock making his requests
"The one who searches would dangle
"The one who wants would tangle
"And a marvel you would know
"From following that old crow."

"And you," said the Demicock to the second, who was older and very wise, "what can you tell us?"

"What every curious man would like to know, but of which your master ought still to be unaware," he said—in gnomish, in order that Melimelo did not understand, but the demicock translated it into French later.

"I'll tell you on the way," he said.

The old gnome continued: "Know that the Beauty didn't kill Chatfourré. "The fay Ouroucoucou, seeing him about to kill Boutonderose, afflicted him with a violent hemorrhage, followed by a sleep so profound that the scoundrel seemed dead. Now, it was him, with Faribolifaribola and Falbalatine, disguised as men, who had robbed Mère Lépargne as she was taking Boutonderose to Melimelo in the dark, to marry her to him, because she knew how good he was and because she loved him.

"The three thieves tied Mère Lépargne to a tree in the Black Forest, and then, seeing that little Recurette, her maidservant, had beautiful teeth, they extracted them in order to replace all those that Faribolifaribola lacked. Then they gave her to the specters of the bad poets to make an Iris, but they reserved Boutonderose in order to cut off her beautiful hair and make a wig for Falbalatine. And Chatfourré declared that he had the intention of using his art to take away all the beauty she had in order to transfer it to Falbalatine, who is so stupid that she believed him, although he was making fun of them.

"Then he took the bay horse and the covered cart, which contained a fine dowry for Boutonderose, to his brother's pretty house, having resolved to kill him during the night in order to take possession of it, for he knew that the pretty house pleased Mère Lépargne a great deal and he promised himself to force her to give him her daughter in marriage.

"However, as Chatfourré, with his two accomplices, was approaching Melimelo's house, Boutonderose, who was in the back of the cart, let herself down to the ground in order to flee. The salamanders perceived that, and ran after her. You know what happened. The salamanders, as cowardly as all evil women, ran away as soon as they hear Melimelo shout, while Chatfourré, cleverer and delighted to be rid of them, introduced himself furtively into his brother's house, counting on being able, during the night, to take possession of the house, the dowry and Boutonderose. But he was mistaken.

"The Beauty, who knew how much Melimelo loved is evil brother, only had him put in the cart in order to send him to the subterrain the Black Forest, where I was to keep him imprisoned until he became better, because the fay Ouroucoucou, at the moment when Boutonderose had laughed while talking to the young man, had let her know that I had run to rescue Mère Lépargne and had brought her into the subterrain.

"All went well until then. If only Melimelo hadn't rhymed at what the enemy gnomes said, who were still holding poor Recurette—for as soon as he rhymed, they took him for one of theirs, who had found the hidden door of the subterrain where Mère Lépargne had left me to guard her treasures and they all came running.

"In the meantime, Falbalatine and Faribolifaribola, who ran away to the home of their friend Lustucru, found a sea around his château, which caused them to take refuge in the Black Forest. The gnome fops received them with delight, and while Mère Lépigne had sent me to rescue Recurette they went into the subterrain, which was open, leaving Falbalatine and

Faribolifaribola in triumph—so that when I came back with Recurette, I no longer found Mère Lépigne, and everything had been pillaged.

"There's no need to tell you the rest; you and your master will liberate her. But a fool sometimes gives good advice—do what the gnome who just left us to run after bats said as he finished his rhymes: follow that crow, which is flying from tree to tree in front of us. I'll observe everything from a distance.

Melimelo and the demirooster followed the crow, which led them into the Elysium of Poets. When they were in the middle of the Black Forest, the demicock said to Melimelo: "Master, I can hear something. I'm going to climb that big oak, in order to discover what it is. But whatever happens, always let me go first, and only follow me a hundred paces behind.

When the demicock had climbed the tallest oak in the forest, he shouted, rhyming involuntarily:

"Master I see a great light.
"Flowing and bright,
"Coming in this direction
"In a terrible collection."

"Is that good or bad, what you're telling me?" shouted Melimelo.

"Master, I'm sick at heart
"I can see the bay and the cart.
"I can hear cries and see tears
"And Lépargne full of fears,
"In distress and morose.
"I see Boutonderose,
"With her beautiful tresses

"Which Falbalatine dresses.
"I see Chatfourré full of joy
"Treating her like a toy,
"With her lovely blonde hair
"Held up in the air."

As the demicock stopped talking, he uttered a loud cock-a-doodle-doo, and the bay horse responded with a loud whinny.

Melimelo was astonished by all that the demicock said. He was seething with impatience to go to the aid of Boutonderose and her mother, but seeing the demirooster hopping with all its might toward the covered cart, making him a sign with its wing not to advance, he was afraid he might spoil everything, and kept a hundred paces behind.

Faribolifaribola, having heard the demicock, started to laugh, saying: "I believe it's the son of that subterranean gnomess that my husband, the sylph Zizizifefefe changed into a cock twenty-five years ago, which made that simpleton Soufflisouflinsoufflot believe that he'd made an immortal cock, although he'd made it as resuscitations are done at the Arepo."

"It's my brother's demicock," said Chatfourré, "which we divided in two, and of which I ate my half."

"You did well," said the salamander.

"Of which you ate half!" cried Mère Lépargne. "Wretch! You asked for my daughter in marriage, and you'd eaten half my son! You'll pay for that!"

At those words, Faribolifaribola gave Mère Lépargne ten slaps, and Falbalatine tweaked Boutonderose' nose—which was short without being snub—as many times, with all her strength. On seeing that, Melimelo entered into such a great fury that he was about to advance and punish her, in spite of what the demicock had said to him—but fortunately, he heard a loud noise, like a river overflowing, and then a great howl, like a furious wolf, and then a loud barking, like a fox yapping while chasing chickens—which made Melimelo stop short.

"Oh, we're doomed!" said the two salamanders. "Here comes the Talking River, the wolf in the gray cloak and the fox with the blue jacket. They've been sent by the fay Ouroucoucou, who lives in the Valley of Fae, to help Lépargne and Boutonderose, who have made her angry with us by their false reports.

"It's necessary to kill the old woman before her friends arrive," said Chatfourré. And he took out a large scalpel with which to cut her throat.

Scarcely had he spoken those evil words, however, than the fay Ouroucoucou, invisible as she was, suspended Mère Lépargne and Boutonderose twenty feet up in the air, while the two animals and the river-fay, who had heard the demirooster's loud cock-a-doodle-doo, came to the rescue. As soon as they saw the salamanders, the wolf knocked Faribolifaribola down; the fox bit Falbalatine's buttocks and the river surrounded the bay horse and the covered cart, threatening to extinguish the two salamanders like candles.

Seeing her enemy on the ground, Mère Lépigne came down and tore off her frills, in which all her power resided, and nothing could any longer be seen but a wretched wrinkled old woman. Then she approached Falbalatine, who tried to run away, and tore off her gauze furbelow, in which all her power was contained, and there was nothing any longer to be seen, instead of a brunette, a bleary-eyed redhead whose freckled face resembled the belly of a toad.

"Let that be your punishment," she said, "for I'm good..."

Then she took the frills and the furbelow and touched Chatfourré's face with them, saying to him: "By the power of the Fay Ouroucoucou, I give you Falbalatine, and I marry you; and every time you cease to burn with amour for her, an ounce of flesh will be cut from you, and if it's her that ceases to love you, the horns of a chamois will grow on your temples."

Falbalatine, in despair, submitted to her fate, but her mother was bursting with rage, for the older the salamanders of the Arepo get, the more malevolent they become.

The demirooster having approached, Mère Lépargne said to him: "My dear son, I'd like to render you your form, but it's necessary first to have the half that this wretch Chatfourré has eaten. Will Melimelo, without whom we can do nothing, consent to that? There he is, always good-hearted, embracing his evil brother..."

Indeed, Melimelo, as soon as he had seen his brother free, had run to him, carried away by fraternal tenderness, saying to him: "Oh, my dear bother, I thought you were dead, and I'm seeing you again!" And he embraced Chatfourré forcefully, whom misfortune rendered impotent. But two large chamois-horns that had just sprouted from his temples nearly put his younger brother's eyes out.

Mère Lépargne, seeing him thus coiffed, started to laugh and laugh, asking him whether he loved his little wife dearly.

"I wish she were a hundred feet underground, or in the river, damn her," relied Chatfourré, angrily. "I'm a handsome man!"

"That can be remedied," Mère Lépargne retorted, "by cutting in flesh the weight of your horns."

Chatfourré liked that idea, and asked Melimelo, who was weeping, to consent to it. He even offered his scalpels and lancets in order to perform the operation. But the fox and the wolf, great experts in such matters, saying that they would take care of it, rid him of his shoulder-blades in less than two minutes. As the fox and the wolf removed the flesh, the horns diminished, and when they were reduced to nothing, the two amputators stopped work.—to their great regret, for it was evident that they were beginning to take pleasure in it.

By means of perlimpinpin powder,[4] which Mère Lépargne put on the incisions, everything was consolidated. In order for Chatfourré to be proportionate to his height, however, it was necessary to reduce it by a foot and a half, so that he was no taller than a small boy—but he was only more malevolent in consequence, because taking away his flesh had taken away none of his malice; and it is since those times that dwarfs have been more malevolent than tall men.

Faribolifaribola said to her daughter: "Look, then, you red-haired bitch, the most salamandrine of the salamanders of the Arepo, at the extract of the husband you've been given!"

"I'd still rather have him than nothing," replied Falbalatine.

While all that was happening, Mère Lépargne, in order to distract Melimelo, who had been moved to too much compassion by his brother's frightful screams,

_____

[4] "Poudre de perlimpinpin" [perlimpinpin powder] was widely adopted in eighteenth century France as a generic term for ineffective medicaments sold by charlatans.

made him a sign to approach the covered cart, to which the fay Ouroucoucou had just returned Boutonderose.

"Oh, Madame," he said, "how many pardons I have to ask of you as well as your lovely daughter. My wrongs surpass those of my brother."

"There's a great difference," replied Boutonderose, blushing.

"Yes, yes, there's a vast one," said Mère Lépargne. "Two poor rhymes aren't such a great evil, especially when one hasn't made bad usage of them, like Untilgreb, who is the Chatfourré of poets. Come on! In spite of the difficulty that Melimelo had caused me, induced into error as he was by the gnomes of the Black Forest, who are scoundrels, gamblers and drunkards, like all lackeys, I want to forget everything, but on one condition."

"Madame," said Melimelo, "I'll submit to anything, and receive in any case the pot of gold coins that I've brought back from Lustucru's house; I make you a present of them. They'll be better in your hands than mine.

"Who found you so much money, my son?"

"It was my demicock, Madame." Melimelo had not understood that the demicock was Mère Lépargne's son.

"Oh, what a good domestic.

"Even if he were an entire cock, as soon as he pleases you, he's yours, Madame."

"You anticipate me, my child; I'm burning with desire to have him."

Melimelo turned round to present his demicock, but instead of the demirooster he saw a handsome young man advance to embrace him.

"Oh, my dear Melimelo!" cried Mère Lépargne, transported by joy. "Your demirooster...is my son! That accursed enchanter of the Arepo, Zizizifefefe, in whom my son had imprudently confided, had changed him into a cock by making him drink the milk of an Arepo sala-mander, which is a powerful poison."

"My good and dear Master," said the handsome Lisdamour, previously the demicock, "I'm the brother of the beautiful Boutonderose; a trifling libertinage caused my misfortune; it was necessary, in order for me to be-come again as you see me now, for a physician to muti-late me; that a jealous lover should warm me in the bos-om of his young mistress, who preferred constancy to beauty; that a sage young man would return me gener-ously to my mother, even though he loved me with all his heart, even though I found him treasures and even though he knew me to have the power to enclose foxes, wolves and rivers in my belly; and finally, in order to have my eaten half, that as much flesh be cut from my eater as he had devoured of mine. All is fulfilled, and Boutonderose is the prize I offer you. If it cost those who consume peoples as dear as it has cost Chatfourré, they'd think twice about it.

"And if their benefactors were well enough com-pensated," said Melimelo, darting a glance at Boutonderose, one would see many more benevolent men."

Chatfourré being cured and diminished, everyone was approximately content. Melimelo, ever sensitive, asked Mère Lépargne to restore Falbalatine's beauty, and even Faribolifaribola's frills, but the fay Ouroucoucou forbade it. Mère Lépargne therefore send the three guilty parties on a boat that the Talking River carried, escorted by the fox in the blue jacket and the wolf in the gray cloak—who both soon regained their human form—to an island in America, where they could live at their ease by working hard.

The following day, Melimelo married Boutonderose, to whom Mère Lépargne gave as a dowry two diamonds of an inestimable value, one set in rubies, which was named *labor*, and the other in a blank setting, named *thrift*. She added a tidy sum of money, lands and châteaux.

On the day of the wedding, the sage gnome brought back Recurette, and as she was a faithful, neat, caring and invariably good-humored domestic servant, Mère Lépargne, in ceding her to her daughter, said: "Here's the best part of your dowry: a good domestic ought to be as dear to her masters as one of their limbs, for she's as useful to them.

The young spouses lived happily together, always attentive to pleasing one another, and having no pleasure unless they shared it. They never dissipated, although they made many charities, for Mère Lépargne always supervised their household, and Recurette served them with affection; with the result that they gave a good dowry to their daughters and left considerable property to their sons.

THE FOUR BEAUTIES AND THE FOUR BEASTS

There was once a family that lived in a pretty house in the middle of a wood, named Charmelieu, or the Red House. It must have been a long way from here, because there were beings in that land who ate people.

The father was named Brancabanda, and the mother Houssihoussa, and they had four sons and four daughters. The boys were tall and sturdy and the girls so very beautiful that no one has ever seen anything to equal them. Their hair was golden, their eyes stars, their cheeks roses, their breasts lilies, and they were so perfect that one would have sworn, on seeing them, that they were fays rather than human creatures. What is more, they knew how to spin, sew and embroider, and they sang like sirens. As for the four boys, they were also very handsome; they had ebony hair, a masculine and proud appearance, tall stature, broad shoulders and slim legs; one might have taken them for Princes rather than for the sons of a modest countryman.

Brancabanda and Houssihoussa were only commoners, but they became so proud, on seeing such children that they no longer wanted their sons to work the land or their daughters to spin. They raised their sons like Messieurs and their daughters like Demoiselles; the girls embroidered and sang all days long, and, as for their brothers, they went hunting, for their father, and especially their mother, had told them only to live like gentlemen, and that way, perhaps they might marry the daughters of lords, who would fall in love with them on seeing them living so nobly, being so handsome and so strong. The mother had also said to the daughters that by embroidering and singing like demoiselles, they might well charm a Comte or a Marquis, who would be only too glad to obtain them in marriage. The result was that their parents rendered them very proud, and scornful of their peers.

Whenever some commoner came to Charmelieu, or even some poor gentleman, Houssihoussa said to her daughters: "Go to your rooms; the sun is too hot today." And the father responded to gallants: "My daughters are too young; goodbye." And the poor gallants went home with death in their hearts, for the girls were so beautiful that one could not see them without dying of love.

Now, for some time, in the neighborhood of the Red House, there had also been a little old woman, wrinkled, hump-backed, bandy-legged and bleary-eyed, named Grignotine,[5] the Lady of La Loge, who also had four sons and four daughters. The boys were so deformed that one could not look at them without horror, and the girls so ugly that one could not see the without feeling nauseated.

The eldest of the boys was Z-shaped and had only one large eye in the middle of his forehead; the second was only two-and-a-half feet tall and resembled Punch; the third was red-haired, cross-eyed and stammered, and his mouth was cleft vertically with a hare-lip; the fourth

---

[5] The French word *grignotine* was not to be found in dictionaries in 1785, although it has since been invented, in order to refer to "snack food." It comes from the verb *grignoter*, "to nibble" and Restif presumably intended to imply a somewhat rodent-like appearance

was one-armed and had a tumor the size of a lemon beneath his left eye. Each of the girls resembled one of her brothers, feature for feature, and if there was any difference, it was that the boys were considerably less ugly than their sisters.

Thus had the noble Fay Ouroucoucou permitted it to be, who had her reasons.

But if the little old woman and her family were ugly, they were rich, and good—so good that, once people got to know them, it was as if their deformity gradually diminished, and they liked them as much as if they had been handsome. They did good deeds throughout the canton, and one never heard talk of anything but their generosity.

One day, while going past the Red House, Grignotine's four sons and four daughters saw through the gaps in the main gate the four daughters and four sons of Brancabanda and Houssihoussa. The boys were playing tennis in the courtyard, while their sisters were embroidering in the shade under a hazel-tree arbor and their mother milked the cows—for she preferred to do it herself rather than let her daughters spoil their hands.

The Grignotins found the girls and boys of the Red House so beautiful and so handsome that they all fell in love, to the extent that they stopped eating and drinking. And the boys said to one another: "We're very lucky to love the daughters of the Red House, who are so proud that they cause people to die of love." But the girls said nothing. And all eight of them grew thin, which was a pity—except for the boy and girl who had tumors, for the growths increased visibly, which did not embellish them.

That gave Grignotine, who did not know what was wrong with them, a great deal of chagrin. Every day, she went to ask them: "My poor children, what's the matter with you?" But they did not reply, for they were utterly ashamed, being so ugly, of being lovesick.

"Oh, it's the ogre of Vaucharme," said the old woman, "who has put a spell on them. If I knew what it was I'd go to Courtenay, to the noble fay Ouroucoucou, my godmother, who would take it off."

In the end, Grignotin pressed them so much, she wept so much, that Caliborgon, her eldest, who was forty years old, replied to his mother, blushing: "My dear Maman, I love Mademoiselle Hhûeip Brancabanda de Charmelieu"—for he had heard that the brothers and sisters named themselves thus while watching them play.

Ratatinet, the second, who was thirty-nine, then said: "And I, my dear Maman, love Mademoiselle Hhûhhuip Brancabanda."

"And I Mademoiselle Bizibizibizi Brancabanda," said Becdelièvre, the third, who was one year younger.

"I love Mademoiselle Hhouiphhouip Brancabanda," said Loupinet, the fourth, who was only thirty-seven.[6]

"Is that all, my children?" Grignotine replied. "Console yourselves; I'll have you marry your mistresses, and I'll go ask for their hands in marriage for you tomorrow."

Grignotine's four sons shook their heads, saying to themselves: *You can ask, but will you obtain them?*

---

[6] Author's note, credited to the hypothetical narrator: "The Burgundians, in telling this tale to their children to put them to sleep, pronounce the first name like the sound of a simple kiss, the second like a double kiss and the fourth like a very emphatic triple kiss. I shall also observe that they leave out many events and recount others of which the blissful ignorance and urbanity of cities do not allow the conservation."

"Well, my daughters," said the old woman then, "Will you also tell me your woes?"

The eldest, Caliborgnette, who was thirty-six years old, hid her face modestly, which would have rendered her very likeable if she had not been so ugly, and started weeping instead of replying.

"And you, Ratatinette?" said the old woman to the second.

Ratatinette's only response was to put her head in her apron, sobbing.

"Will you talk to me, then, Becdehaze?" said Grignotine to the third.

Becdehaze ran away to hide.

"It's up to you, then, Loupinette," said the mother to her youngest daughter, aged thirty-three. "Come on, little girl, I want someone to obey me."

But Loupinette stated crying with all her might, and her mother, seeing the tumor growing prodigiously, was obliged to employ many caresses to appease her.

"I'll wager that it's also amour," Grignotine said, to herself—and, seeing that her daughters made no reply, she became certain of it.

"Is it the Seigneur des Vauxgermains?"

"They're black monks, Mother."

"Is it the Seigneur des Boislabbés?"

"They're monks, Mother.

"Is it the Seigneur de Saintcyr?"

"They're white monks, Mother."

"Is it the Seigneur de Lichères?"

"They're monks, Mother."

"Then it's de Nitri?"

"Monks, Mother."

"De Saci?"

"Canons, Mother."

"Escerf?"

"Black and white monks, Mother."

"I'll wager that it's the de Charmelieu lads?"

The daughters did not say a word.

"That's it, then! Have courage, my daughters. While asking for the sisters for your brothers, I'll propose you for the boys of the Red House. Each of you, just name me the one you like best."

Then Caliborgnette said: "Sacripar," Ratatinette "Fandipouf," Becdehaze, "Farôdor" and Loupinette "Craquoman."

"It shall be done," said the old woman, "or my name will no longer be Grignotine."

The next day, Grignotine put on her beautiful yellow-and-green satin dress, her skirt the color of dead leaves, her scarlet cape, her black taffeta hat, her sapphire pendants, her chrysoprase necklace and her duck-egg-blue velvet shoes embroidered with mother-of-pearl. She had her russet donkey saddled and she went straight to the Red House, the home of Brancabanda.

She was well enough received, except that the brothers and sisters could not help laughing a little at her face and her adornment, but the sisters looked at the nacre of her shoes, which they thought quite beautiful. When she had rested she was asked what she wanted and what they could do for her.

"I am the Lady of La Loge," said Grignotine, and I've come to propose to you four good, young and rich gentlemen for the four beautiful daughters that you have here."

"Many thanks—for we know that La Loge is a good and rich fief."

"That's not all," she continued; "those four gentlemen have for sisters four young demoiselles of the finest character, the most virtuous in the canton; we shall render you as much as you give, if you wish."

The thanks were doubled, and the young men started to lavish a thousand politenesses on the old lady. They gave her dinner, and she went home joyfully, to tell her children that everything was going well.

Caliborgnon and Caliborgnette shook their heads, for neither the brothers nor the sisters had any vanity.

"What does that mean?" Grignotine said to them.

"Maman," replied the eldest daughter, "it's just that Monsieur Brancabanda's sons and daughters don't know us."

"What! They don't know you! And you love them without knowing them! But there's no harm done. Tomorrow you'll visit your mistresses, each with a present that I'll give you to take them. In the meantime, rejoice, for sadness spoils beauty and joy even embellishes ugliness."

And they set about rejoicing—but no matter how hard they tried, they were no more beautiful for it.

The following day, Grignotine had her sons put on their best clothes, which she had kept for more than twenty years in a beautiful wooden chest, well waxed, for they only put them on at the great annual festivals. They were in iron-gray cloth with black buttons as big as goose-eggs; their boots were knee-length and their coat-tails so broad and so stiff that they made the poor Grognotins liked like strutting turkey-cocks.

When they were dressed, their Mother said: "Oh, my sons, you're as handsome as angels; but that's not sufficient. Here are the presents that I've destined for your mistresses. You, Caliborgnon, take this lovely white dog; you, Ratatinet, this domesticated gray wolf; you, Becdelièvre, this large black cock; and you, Loupinet, this red sheep. You'll present your gifts as soon as you've asked for the daughters, and you'll listen carefully to what's said to you, so that you can report it back to me word for word. And whatever is said to the first who speaks, the others must still ask for their mistresses."

The four brothers were encouraged by their mother's speech. They set forth together, each leading his present on a leash.

They had not gone a quarter of a league when, on the little hill of Puitsdebond, they met four braggarts, whistling, chatting, blaspheming, swearing, shouting and playing the fool. They were the sons of Charmelieu, Sacripar, Fandipouf, Farôdor and Craquoman, who were coming to see Caliborgnette, Ratatinette, Becdehaze and Loupinette, their sisters. The four sons of Charmelieu saw the four Grignotins at a distance, and stated laughing, pointing at them and mocking them—which rendered the poor Grignotins deeply ashamed.

When they came closer, Sacripar, bold as he was, was so fearful of them that he threw a stone at them and ran away; Fandipouf hit them with his cane; Farôdor wanted to make them dance and threw their hats on the ground; and Craquoman said: "We might as well amuse ourselves with them! They're apes, and I've seen similar ones in the Congo during my last voyage to Germany."

"They have a fine dog!" said Sacripar.

"A fine wolf!" said Fandipouf.

"A fine cock," said Farôdor.

"A fine sheep!" said Craquoman.

"It's necessary to take them! It's necessary to take them," cried the four brothers, "in order to present them to our mistresses."

"Let's see! I'll begin," said Sacripar.

"I want the gray wolf," said Fandipouf.

"And I the black cock," said Farôdor.

"And I the red sheep," said Craquoman.

Scarcely had Sacripar put his hand on the white dog, however, than it bit him hard enough to draw blood. The wolf showed its teeth to Fandipouf; the cock started leaping at Farôdor's eyes, and the sheep, having retreated twenty paces, butted Craquoman so terribly that he threw him into the air—which made the four Brancabandas go away, cursing.

In the meantime, the poor Grignotins picked up their hats, and fled as quickly as they could, looking behind them at intervals. But the youngest called out to the Brancabandas: "Messieurs, Messieurs, turn right, for on the left, past Le Croixpilate, there's the ogre of Vaucharme, who eats people."

"You're apparently his sons," relied Sacripar.

"They ought to be strung up," said Fandipouf.

"Let's go see this ogre," put in Farôdor.

"I'll kill him myself," exclaimed Craquoman.

And they turned left, instead of right—but they soon got scared, and went back to the road that Loupinet had indicated to them.

Meanwhile, the four Grignotins continued on their way, and at midday they arrived at Charmelieu, at the home of Brancabanda, whom they found sitting in the shade outside his door.

As soon as he had seen them in the distance, the fellow had called his wife and his daughters, saying: "Come and see these little apes, with four animals, which are coming on their own, without guides. I'd like to know who makes them dance..."

Houssihoussa had come quickly, with her daughters—and while the Brancabanda family were staring at them, the Grignotins arrived. But when the four beauties had seen them at close range, they were so frightened that they fled to their rooms.

"Monsieur and Madame," said the eldest. "Is this not the Red House of Charmelieu, and are you not Monsieur Brancabanda and Madame Houssihoussa?"

"Yes," replied the father of the four beauties, laughing.

"My name, Monsieur and Madame, is Caliborgnon, at your service. Madame Grignotine, my mother, came yesterday to have the honor of saluting you and to ask you for the hand in marriage of Mademoiselle Hhûeip, your eldest daughter."

"You can't think so!" said Brancabanda. "You frightened her!"

"I know, Monsieur," Caliborgnon replied, "that I'm not handsome; but inquire about myself and my brothers in the canton; I don't believe anyone will speak ill of us. In addition, my mother has given me this fine white dog, to give you as a present."

"Let him keep his dog," replied Houssihoussa. "I don't want to give him my daughter."

Caliborgon tried to insist, but the mother of the four beauties flew into a temper. "I'd rather have your dog for a son-in-law than you," she said to him, scornfully.

Immediately, Caliborgnon began to weep, and was no more handsome for it.

After presenting himself, Ratatinet said: "Monsieur and Madame, my name is Ratatinet; my mother has permitted me to ask you for the hand in marriage of the beautiful Hhûhhuip, your second daughter, and to offer you as a present this domesticated gray wolf."

"I can't accept it," said Brancabanda.

"Let him keep his wolf!" cried the mother. "Wolf as it is, I'd rather give him my daughter than that scoundrel.

Ratatinet stepped back immediately, his heart swollen, saying: "Inquire about me, Madame, and you'll see that people will tell you..."

As soon as he had finished speaking, Becdelièvre was seen to come forward, timidly. "Monsieur and Madame, my name is Becdelièvre, the third son of Grignotine, who spoke to you yesterday, and I've come to ask you for the hand in marriage of the beautiful Bizibizibizi, asking you to accept this fine black cock, which my mother has asked me to present to you."

"We have enough cocks for our hens, Ugly Mug," said Houssihoussa; "I'd rather give my daughter in marriage to a cock than to you."

Becdelièvre immediately withdrew, with tears in his eyes, saying to himself. "Alas, I've never said harsh things to anyone, but I've just received some very cruel ones!"

Finally, Loupinet presented himself, with his red sheep; but Houssihoussa did not give him time to explain himself. "What does this ruffian want? Your red sheep, because of its rarity, is worth a hundred times more than you."

While she said that, Loupinet still recited, like his brothers: "My name is Loupinet, the youngest son of Grignotine, and I've come to ask you for the hand in marriage of the beautiful Hhouiphhouip, your fourth daughter."

"I'd rather give her to your sheep," replied Houssihoussa, again—and poor Loupinet withdrew, sighing.

Thus refused, the four brothers went home, utterly ashamed, without even being offered anything to drink. When they reached the Le Croixpilate fork, where they had encountered the Brancabanda brothers in the morning, they were so deeply afflicted that, without perceiving it, they took the road that led to Vaucharme, the home of the ogre Carnicroquain, who ate people.

They walked for a long time without saying anything. In the end, they realized that they had gone astray and that they were in the valley of Vaucharme, but by the time they noticed it, it was too late.

They saw a peasant-woman in a field spreading dung. "Where are you going, my lads?"

"To La Loge, Mother."

"Alas, no: it's to the home of the ogre of Vaucharme; run away quickly, so that he doesn't see you, for he'll eat you."

"He doesn't eat you, then, Mother?"

"No my lads, I'm too old and too tough. Save yourselves, for if he sees you, he'll attract you with his breath, as a snake attracts birds."

The four Grignotins wanted to get away, but they were so tired and weak that they were unable to run, so the ogre perceived them and he drew them to him with his breath.

"Come in, come in!" he cried to them, in ogrish— which is a very harsh language, even harsher than German. "Here's a chubby little one," he added, touching Loupinet's tumor, "who'll make me a nice meal. Who are you, for I like to know what I'm eating?"

"Alas, we're the four boys of La Loge, sons of the good lady Grignotine."

"The sons…?" said the ogre, going pale.

"Of the good lady Grignotine, most amiable of ogres!"

"You're the sons…! Come in, Messieurs, come in. Be welcome."

"Alas," said Caliborgnon, "eat us straight away, if you wish, for we're so unhappy that one misfortune more wouldn't make any difference."

"Good!" said the ogre, smiling from ear to ear. "You're the first ones who have ever engaged me to eat them, except for an Englishman who came here expressly from his own country in order to beg me to give him a sepulcher in my stomach. He was quite content, for I expedited him in a single meal, of which nothing was left that was larger than a lentil. As for you, however, I won't render you the same service, and I'm not in a humor to be obliging every day. Sit down there with your animals; I'll give you some milk, butter and cheese. I have many other things to, including a very tender thigh of…"

"Of, God!" cried Ratatinet, "Don't finish! You'll cause our death, and if you don't want to eat us, let us live!"

"So be it," said the ogre. "Everyone had his own tastes, and I don't condemn anyone's. But I want you to eat what I'm going to serve you, otherwise I'll set before you…"

"We'll eat it, we'll eat it, handsome ogre," said Becdelièvre, swiftly.

And they ate the cheese and butter and drank the first-rate milk of she-wolves and wild sows, which fortified them considerably. They even felt, after that meal,

99

that they could have eaten a little meat, but their good education combated that carnivorous inclination.

When they were well-refreshed and well-rested, Carnicroquain told them that they could leave. They were burning with desire to do so, for the she-wolf milk, in giving them the desire to eat, had taken away that of being eaten. They got up, therefore, each taking his animal, and left.

They had not yet got out of the ogre's courtyard when they heard voices singing, and others that were crying out, and one that sounded like their mother's, lamenting. They stopped, as motionless as boundary-markers.

Carnoquain started laughing with all his might, saying: "Oh, a fine windfall, a fine windfall! But hide, the four of you; I want those fellows to be caught in my snare." And he hid them in his slaughterhouse, were there was only one tiny window.

As soon as they were hidden, they saw the four Brancabandas arrive, leading Grignotine on her donkey, with her head turned toward its tail, and making her four daughters march to either side of her, all disheveled. At that spectacle, the four Grignotins thought they would die of dolor.

"Oh, you old witch," said Sacripar, "you come to our house to mock my father, my mother, my sisters and us…!"

Fandipouf said: "We've met your apes—oh, if we had known who they were! But perhaps we'll find them again at our house, or on the road."

"A fine family!" said Farôdor. "And they wanted to ally themselves with ours!"

As for Craquotin, he promised nothing less than to exterminate all the Grignotins in the world, even if there were a hundred thousand.

"My lads," Grignotine, "You're wrong to mistreat me, and even more wrong to act so brutally with young women as honest as my daughters; fortune sometimes changes, at the moment when one least expects it, and one is obliged to adore what one has scorned."

"In the name of humanity," said Becdehaze, "respect my mother, our sex and yourselves!"

Farôdor responded by spitting in her face.

Becdehaze wiped it away, and said to him, softly: "Can one act with so much fury against oneself? Oh, Farôdor, is that the price of the sentiments I have for you...?"

The four Grignotins wept, not daring to move.

"Oh, the wretches!" exclaimed Carnicroquain. "I'm not the most tender of individuals, and yet I feel touched by compassion almost as often as I'm seized by fury. You're going to see a fine game!"

Meanwhile, the four brothers said: "Let's see what there is in that château, and whether the girls there are beautiful."

Carnicroquain, who heard that, caused four of his provisions to appear, as white as lilies, who were due to be eaten the following day at a great feast that he intended to give his friends Brisecrâne, Massacrotin and Cassechine.

As soon as the four brothers perceived the four beauties they ran to force the door of the château. Carnicroquain had opened it by a crack, and was only retaining it with his back. The four brothers set about trying to break it down, with no more success than if it had been a wall.

Carnicroquain, counterfeiting the voice of a decrepit old man, shouted: "What do you want, my lads? I'm just a poor old man, who lives here in solitude with my granddaughters, to protect them from rogues. Pass on, pass on, and don't come to afflict my poor old age."

"Open up, you old ape!" cried Farôdor.

"Open up right away!" added Sacripar.

"We're going to amuse ourselves a little with your daughters," said Fandipouf.

"We've got a pretty one here, to whom we're going to marry you!" shouted Craquoman.

"You absolutely insist, then?" replied Carnicroquain.

"You ought to have done it already!" retorted Fandipouf.

"You ought to know..." At the same time, he let go of the door and stood aside. The four brothers all rushed in at once.

"Wretches!" cried Carnicroquain, in a thunderous voice.

The four brothers saw a giant more than twelve feet tall, and fell backwards, gripped by fear. Carnicroquain grabbed all four of them, tied them up like a bundle of asparagus and took them to his kitchen, where he put them on a plank. Then, returning to Grignotine and her daughters, he invited them in, gave them milk, butter and cheese and brought out Caliborgon, Ratatinet, Becdelièvre and Loupinet, which gave Grignotine and her daughters even more pleasure.

"What vengeance would you like?" asked Carnicroquain.

"None, alas," replied Grignotine. "Release them and let them go."

"No, by the jawbone of my father, the great Broyelesos!" said Carnicroquain. At the same time, he went to fetch the four Brancabanda brothers, untied them and showed them his tomahawk. "You can be killed and eaten right now, or you can adore these young beauties, and say nice things to them, with which they'll be content, as will I."

Trembling with fear, the four brothers threw themselves to their knees, Sacripar before Caliborgnette, Fandipouf before Ratatinette, Farôdor before Becdehaze and Craquoman before Loupinette, and they started begging their pardon.

Beautiful Caliborgnette/Ratatinette/Becdehaze/Loupinette," they said, in unison, "forgive us for our folly. How blind we must have been not to see that you're adorable! What eyes! What a mouth! What teeth! What a nose! What a figure! What..."

"That's enough details," Grignotine interrupted, laughing.

"The four lovers continued: "Receive my homage; yes I adore you; I invest my glory and my happiness in obtaining you for a wife, and I promise to oblige my father and my mother, by giving my sisters to your bothers. What an alliance!—and how much astonishment it will excite!"

"That's not all," said the ogre. "Come on, Messieurs, down on all fours, so that these ladies can climb on to your backs, and take them home."

They obeyed very swiftly, for they already wanted to be out of the house of the terrible son of the great Broylesos.

"You're heaping me with favors," Grignotine said to Carnicroquain, "but I have a favor to ask you, nevertheless, which is to stop eating people and give me the four naked girls that I saw in your kitchen."

The ogre trembled from head to toe at that request. "Madame," he said to Grognotine, "I believe that I've done enough to merit your benevolence, but you want to take away my greatest privilege!"

"That's because there's no happiness without virtue," Grignotine replied to him, "and I want to make you loved. Try it."

"I'm forced to do as you ask," he said in a low voice, "for I saw right away that you're a friend of the noble fay of Courtenay, the great Ouroucoucou. Command—but how shall I regale my three friends tomorrow?"

"I'll tell you. My sons, what response was made to you when you asked for your mistresses? Everything depends on that."

Houssihoussa replied to me that she would rather have my white dog as a son-in-law than me," said Caliborgnon.

"She shall have him."

"My gray wolf than me," said Ratatine.

"She shall have him."

"My black cock than me," said Becdelièvre.

"She shall have him."

"My red sheep than me," said Loupinet.

"She shall have him," and Grignotine, again. "Here, Carnicroquain, you see these four animals that I gave to my sons this morning in order to make a present of them to Brancabanda and Houssihoussa. I abandon them to you. Kill them, and take off their skins, which you'll return to me. You can give the white dog to Brisecrâne, the gray wolf to Massacrotin, the red sheep to Cassechine, and you can have the black cock. Henceforth, don't eat human flesh any more, and we'll be friends. Bitter virtue, as you've just seen, gives me very little power over humans, but it submits beings of your species and all of nature to the noble fay Ouroucoucou."

"I know that only too well. And all four—my three colleagues and I—will obey the great Ouroucoucou. Alas, we are the last of the ogres, and this will be the end of our reign. With what will nurses frighten children?"

"There are other stupidities enough," replied Grignotine.

Carnicroquain, obliged to obey the secret power of the noble fay, first took the white dog in order to kill it, but having looked at it he said, muttering—for he was no fool: "It's a pity!" Then he took the gray wolf, the black cock and the red sheep, repeating; "It's a pity…it appears that my friends and I will have a sad feast tomorrow."

"Take off their skins, then," said Grignotine—and the ogre started skinning them, including the cock, with an infinite dexterity, for ogres excel in that.

A prodigy, however! The flayed skins stood uptight on their feet and continued walking, for the animals only had an outer layer, like our fops, and an appearance of sentiment, which they owed to a foreign power. And Carnicroquain, to his great regret, only found inside the dog, instead of flesh, a sack of wheat; nothing in the wolf but a sack of chestnuts; nothing in the cock but a sack of barley; and nothing in the red sheep but a bundle of asparagus, three bundles of turnips, six cabbages, two bushels of beans and a hundred crabapples.

"With that, you and your friends won't die of hunger," said Grignotine, laughing. And she took the four skins.

As soon as she had them she gave the skin of the white dog to Caliborgnon, that of the gray wolf to Loupinet, that of the black cock to Ratatinet and that of the red sheep to Becdelièvre;[7] the first became a handsome blond-haired man, the second a handsome chestnut-haired man, the third a handsome dark-haired man and the fourth a handsome red-haired man whose head resembled a ruby.

As soon as the Grignotins were handsome, the fay Ouroucoucou, who did not want their ugliness to be lost, gave it to the four boys from Charmelieu, so that Sacripar became Caliborgnon, Fandipouf Becdelièvre, Farôdor Ratatinet and Craquoman Loupinet.

But the four Bracabandas had no sooner become ugly than the four Grignotines became, Caliborgnette a beautiful blonde, Loupinette a beautiful girl with ash-blonde hair, Ratanette a beautiful brunette and Becdehaze a charming redhead with a head like a carbuncle, which was so beautifully scented that one might have thought that Eau Carmes[8] had been poured all over it.

And as soon as the four Grignotines were beautiful, the fay Ouroucoucou, who did not want their ugliness to be lost, sent it to the four girls of Charmelieu. The eldest,

---

[7] I have retained this list as it appears in the original, although it is inconsistent with other passages of the narrative, in which the four skins have been distributed as one might expect, in order of age; the same is true of the lists in the following two paragraphs.

[8] Author's note: "The Burgundians say that 'she had crushed musk-roses in her hands.'" *Eau de Carmes* was an extract of lemon balm and other herbs first produced by Carmelite nuns in the fourteenth century and subsequently marketed as a herbal remedy and cleansing agent.

who was getting dressed, was the first to become ugly. As mirrors had not yet unvented they were looking at themselves in their *repassoir*.[9]

"My God," she said to her younger sister, "I believe that I'm seeing things. Look at my face."

"Oh my God, how ugly you are!"

"Oh, my God, you're frightful!" said the third.

"You're horrific," said the youngest.

"What about you, then?" retorted the eldest.

All three of them looked at themselves; they rubbed the *repassoir*, but the more they rubbed it the more frightful they found themselves. They called their mother, who, having come running, tried to drive them out with thrusts of her spindle, saying to them: "Get out, she-apes; you might frighten my daughters." But, the four girls having started to weep and to speak, their mother recognized their voices.

They told her about the misfortune that had just overtaken them, and as soon as Houssihoussa heard everything, she started screaming, tearing her hair and banging her head against the walls, saying: "Alas, alas, how unfortunate I am! What will their brothers say when they come back! Perhaps it's that damnable old woman from yesterday who's the cause of it, for she looked like a witch..."

In the meantime, Grignotine, well content, went back to La Loge with her sons, her daughters and the four Brancabandas, who were all crestfallen, taking with

---

[9] Author's note: "A kind of large stand bearing a plate of polished brass, which women used to put on their underwear before the invention of hand-mirrors; they can still be seen in the provinces."

her the four young women that the ogre had been going to eat, half a dozen more that he was fattening, and two or three dozen disobedient little boys, whom he had found playing truant—and since that time there have been no ogres nor ogresses, for the last four were not married.

They all arrived at La Loge that evening, where Grignotine made her sons-in-law welcome—for although they had become ugly, her daughters were so good and tender that they did not love them any less, to the extent that they stayed with them gladly, with anyone being able to recognize them.

Poor Brancabandra and Houssihoussa, however, not seeing them arrive in the evening, became very anxious and chagrined.

"Misfortunes never come alone," said the father. "Our daughters have become ugly, and our sons must have been eaten by the ogre of Vaucharme."

The next day they were even more chagrined, and the day after they lamented, for the rumor had spread for ten leagues round that the four boys from Charmelieu had been eaten by ogres because of their bravado, which meant that everyone became so frightened that they deserted Puitsdebond, Le Croixpilate, Vaugermains, Saintcyr, Lichères, Nitry, Sacy and all the other surrounding lands, all the way to Aigremont, and there was no one any longer to be found in the entire canton.

"Alas, alas," said Houssihoussa, "where can we run now that out daughters are horrors of nature? No one will even want us for servants. If there's a poor cowherd somewhere who wants to marry one of them, and will help us to make a living..."

But she had a great deal about which to complain; no one wanted or dared to come to Charmelieu, nor to the surrounding area. When it was necessary to buy clothes or shoes she had to go to the town of Chablis to buy them.

One morning, Houssihoussa climbed on to her donkey and went there with her four daughters, who were greatly ashamed. She had turned up their collars and put aprons over their shoulders as mantles, like Bohemians in order to hide them; but people recognized their voices and everyone looked at them. Women started to laugh at them, for the replies that the father and mother had made to the Grignotins were known and soon, sometimes to one or another of them, they said:

"Is your mother going to marry you to a white dog soon, Hhûeip? My word, that's all your worth now!" or "with a gray wolf, Hhûhhuip?" or "with a black cock, Bizibizibizi?" or "with a red sheep, Hhouiphhouip?"

As for the boys, they followed them, wagging their tongues and saying all kinds of nasty things, and acting very badly—on seeing which, poor Houssihoussa was so broken-hearted that she promised herself never to return to the town, even if she had to go about stark naked and walk without shoes.

When she had returned to Charmelieu, she told her husband all that. "Alas, alas," she said, "everyone is mocking us instead of commiserating with our misfortune"—and her husband hid his face in his hands, without replying, so oppressed was he by shame and chagrin; and the daughters started to weep.

Brancabanda and his wife soon repented of their pride, which was the cause of the fact that no one felt sorry for them and everyone was quite content with their misfortune.

"Oh," said the father, "if I still had Bousselabale, our great lout of a swineherd, whom I sacked because he was too clumsy, I'd give him my eldest daughter Hhûeip in marriage, who's of age and in need of a husband..."

So, Brancabanda repented of his vanity and that of his wife, which had made them refuse their daughters to honest men and bring up their sons badly. To augment his pain, the girls, desolate at their ugliness, wept all day long, and his wife quarreled with him, although she was the more culpable, and flew into rages. In consequence, he left the house at daybreak, as men do who have malevolent wives, and did not return until dusk. As there was no inn in which to while away his chagrin, though, he had to work.

As he worked he said: "Alas, alas! Have I only nourished four sons, the most handsome men in the canton, for the cuisine of ogres? Alas, alas, did I only have four daughters as beautiful as the day and as dexterous as fays for a satanic old woman to witch hem and make them ugly? Unless it was the fay Ouroucoucou, for I remember that my wife went past her one day without curtsying, and those ladies are very susceptible! If I knew that for sure I'd go to her tower in the valley of the Fae,[10] which is so somber that one can scarcely see there in broad daylight, and I'd beg her for mercy! Alas, alas, how unfortunate I am—and my wife still rages at me!"

And the poor fellow wept as he toiled, without receiving consolation from anyone; but those were still his better times.

---

[10] Author's note: "Fae is there by corruption; it's the Vallée-de-la-Fée. It is heavily wooded. One can still see the tower on the hillside, a short distance from the road to Saintcyr at Iranci." In fact, "fae" is sometimes to be found in English prior to 1785 as an equivalent of the French fée, as is fey.

Grignotine did not take long to discover how much poor Brancabanda had to complain about; she was so touched that that she said a few words about it to the fay Ouroucoucou.

The noble fay went invisibly to Charmelieu, so she saw for herself that he no longer had any pride, especially in his daughters, who supported their misfortune patiently and even consoled their mother and father, saying to them: "We're ugly, but in fifty years, wouldn't we have been anyway? Beauty passes, but a good heart remains..." Which gave the noble fay so much pleasure that she resolved to soothe them.

So, one day when Brancabanda was alone in his garden, which was only enclosed by a living hedge, occupied in planting cabbages, thinking about his poor daughters, so ugly that they scared people, and how he was going to marry them off—which was rendering him even more chagrin than usual—a beautiful white dog leapt over the hedge and came to him to be stroked. Brancabanda was afraid, but the white dog started gamboling; it wagged its tail, stood up on its hind legs, put its front paws on the fellow's shoulders and embraced him wholeheartedly. Somewhat reassured by that politeness, Brancabanda said: "What do you want, handsome dog?"

Without responding, even though it could talk very well, the dog went into the house, where it frightened the four daughters and their mother even more, but it caressed them so much that they were soon emboldened and passed their hands over its back, stroking it.[11] When

---

[11] Author's note, credited to "the editor": "It appears that this tale is the source from which Madame de Villeneuve derived that of "The Beauty and the Beast," of which Monsieur

the white dog had domesticated them, it stood up on its hind legs, put one of its forepaws in the hand of the caliborgness Hhûeip, the eldest of the four sisters, and led her to her father, who had stayed in the garden and who did not know what had become of the white dog.

Brancabanda was very surprised to see the white dog leading his daughter by the hand like a bride. "What are you doing, handsome dog?"

Half-yapping and half-talking, the white dog replied: "Monsieur. I would like the beautiful Hhûeip, your eldest daughter, in marriage."

"Beautiful!" said Brancabarda, shaking his head. "One can't argue with tastes, but it cannot be, handsome dog, for you're an animal and I'm a man."

"Qualities count for nothing Monsieur; what does it matter, if I make your daughter happy? You'll have the proof of that the first time you come to see our household in the city of Cynopolis, or Dogville, of which I'm the Marquis and sovereign, for I'm a descendant of the canine god Anubis. Consent, then."

Marmontel made such fortunate use in giving us *Zémire et Azor*. Perhaps even Monsieur de Voltaire profited from it for the denouement of one of his most agreeable works." The original version of "La Belle et la bête," by Gabrielle-Suzanne Barbot de Villeneuve, which is a long novella not based on a folktale, was first published in 1740; a much-abridged plagiarism dating from 1756 is the one more commonly reproduced, but Restif was obviously familiar with the original, perhaps having read the 1765 reprint. The operatic version *Zémire et Azor* (1771), with a libretto by Marmontel and music by André Grétry, as a great success and helped enormously to secure the basic story's enduring popularity.

"Handsome dog, you might be a very respectable gentleman among dogs, but still, you're not of our species; I can't."

"Well, watch me go then."

At the same time, the green dog[12] picked up the girl in his mouth, without her putting up the slightest resistance, set her on his back, leapt over the hedge, and disappeared in no time.

Brancabanda immediately went to recount the misfortune to his wife Houssihoussa, who started to weep, saying: "Alas, alas, my poor daughter, as white as a lily, as red as a rose, as tender as dew! Have I treated her so delicately, then, only for a dog to tear her apart?" For although her daughters were very ugly, and people could not look at them without saying "ugh!" she made a semblance of still finding them as they had been before, and told herself that it would come back. "If I were a man, I wouldn't have let her be carried away. The women of Chablis are going to say to me: 'Alas, alas, having a dog as a son-in-law after refusing gentlemen!'"

"Cam down," said her husband. "He hasn't taken her to do her any harm."

"Oh yes," said his wife, weeping even more copiously. 'He has fangs like a wild boar! And even if he doesn't eat her, with what will he nourish her?"

And she wept, and wept, and wept.

---

[12] In the original version there is a long break in the story before the beginning of this sentence, which only resumes in the subsequent volume, in the interim, that author evidently decided to change the color of the dog, the wolf and the cock, and also to have forgotten the dog's alleged residence in Cynopolis.

Brancabanda was very sad to see his wife weeping waling and grieving. "I think," he said, "that if you put him through what you sometimes put me through, the big green dog would have been frightened and he would have left our poor Hhûeip." And as he saw that she was about to lose her temper with him, he went back into his garden and resumed planting his cabbages.

He had not finished his row when a huge yellow wolf leapt over the hedge and came to place itself beside Brancabanda and lick his hands. He was terrified, and thought he was a dead man, but he was gradually reassured, and, seeing the submissive attitude of the wolf, he said, trembling: "Handsome wolf, what do you want?"

The yellow wolf, without replying, although it could talk very well, went into the house, where it frightened the three daughters and their mother even more than the big green dog had done. They fell backwards, all trembling; but it immediately started licking their hands, so that after a few minutes, they were only half as frightened. And the wolf stood up on its hind legs, put its right forepaw in the left hand of Mademoiselle Hhûhhuip, the second daughter, who dared not refuse it, and led her, half-dead with fear, to her father, without Houssihoussa breathing a word.

Brancabanda was very surprised to see the yellow wolf leading his daughter by the hand like a bride.

"What are you doing, handsome wolf?"

The wolf, half-howling and half-talking, replied: "Monsieur, I would like the beautiful Hhûhhuip, your second daughter, in marriage."

Brancabanda was so frightened that he replied: "That does us great honor, Monsieur, for I have no doubt that among Messieurs the wolves, you're a very fine gentleman, just as the big green dog, my son-in-law, who has just espoused my eldest daughter, is among the dogs."

"You're correct, Monsieur," the yellow wolf replied, mildly. "I descend from a king named Lycaon, who was changed into a wolf for some escapade, which means that I'm treated as a Duc by all my fellows. Your daughter will be the Duchesse de Lycopolis, otherwise Wolfville, as you'll see the first time you visit our household."

"Oh, Seigneur Wolf, if only you were at least of our species...and my daughter were still as she was not so long ago!"

"I'm content with her," said the yellow wolf, showing his teeth as if to laugh. At the same time, he took his wife in his mouth, leapt over the hedge, and had reached the woods in the blink of an eye.

Brancabanda went once again to relate that new misfortune to his wife, but she already knew, for she had seen everything from the door to the garden with her two daughters, without daring to enter it. She started weeping, saying: "Alas, alas, my poor Hhûhhuip, as white as a lily, as red as a rose, as tender as dew. Have I only raised you so delicately to see a wolf to chew you up one day? Alas, alas, to have a wolf for a son-in-law, after having refused so many worthy gentlemen!"

"They would be hard pressed at present," said Brancabanda. "Come, come, those fellows appear to me to be honest folk of their species, and our daughters are perhaps better married than with brutal men like some I've know."

"Yes, yes," said his wife, "here you are again with your crack-brained ideas. And if he doesn't chew her up, on what will he nourish her? Oh, if I were a man, I'd

115

have taken my rifle and I'd have killed that vile yellow wolf."

Pretending to be more resolute than he was, Brancabanda said: "Calm down, wife. I know more than you do. My son-in-law the yellow wolf descends from a King Limaçon, whom I don't know, and my son-in-law the green dog, who descends from Opubis,[13] are fine gentlemen among the wolves and the dogs, for they told me so..."

Shrewish as she was, Houssihoussa had nothing to reply to that; she went back to plying her spindle with her two remaining daughters, and Brancabanda went back to planting his cabbages.

He had not finished the third row when he heard a cock crow, whose cock-a-doodle-doo was so loud that it could be heard for ten leagues around, and all the birds that were flying in the air or chirping in the trees fell down, stunned.

Brancabanda stood up in order to look for the strange cock, and a blue cock as big as an ostrich flew over the hedge and came toward him, flapping its wings so forcefully that the wind it made caused all the apples, pears and plums in the garden to fall. He was afraid; he had never seen such a cock; it was taller than a giraffe and its crest resembled a fine red banner.

It started scratching the soil, rubbing its belly thereon, and making it fly so high above its wings that one might have thought it a swarm of bees. Then it approached Brancabanda with an expression so very ro-

---

[13] The author inserts a note here, credited to "the editor" which is possibly incomplete: "This is the way that Burgundians pronounce." Any French reader would know that "Limaçon" means "snail," and the derivation of "Opubis" is obvious.

guish that the reassured it: "Handsome cock, what do you want?"

The cock, half crowing and half talking, replied, softening its voice a good deal: "Where is the beautiful Bizibizinizi, your third daughter?"

"Yes, beautiful—there's the dampener! She's indoors, with her mother, spinning flax. Handsome cock, leave her be..."

But the cock was already in the house, where it found the cross-eyed Bizibizibizi spinning flax. It walked around her three times, rubbing a wing on the floor, according to the custom of cocks when they want to pay court, and, half-crowing and half-speaking, it said to Houssihoussa: "Good woman, your husband has told me that Bizibizibizi, your third daughter, is here, and I've come to ask you for her in marriage...."

But Houssihoussa, who was not as frightened of a blue cock as tall as a giraffe as she was of a yellow wolf, took her spindle and started flapping it at the bird angrily in order to chase it way, saying: *Chit, chit, chit!*"— seeing which, the cock retreated four steps and lowered its head, rolling its eyes and scratching the floor, like cocks that want to fight, and got ready to leap at her face, which frightened he two girls greatly.

Seeing that the cock was not playing games, Houssihoussa said: "Handsome cock a blue as litmus, it's my husband who married my other two daughters to a big green dog, son of Opubis, and a big yellow wolf, son of King Limaçon; you can go find him, so that he can marry the third to a blue cock with a red crest, son of I don't know who..."

The blue cock did not need telling twice; it extended a wing to the beautiful Bizibizibizi and took her by the hand to her father, like a bride.

"What are you doing, handsome cock?"

"I want this beauty, your third daughter, in marriage."

"That does us great honor, Monsieur, for I have no doubt that among Messieurs the cocks, you're a very fine gentleman, as my son-in-law the big green dog, who descends from King Opubis, is among the dogs, as my son-in-law, the son of the wolf King Limaçon, also my son-in-law, is among the wolves."

"Monsieur," said the blue cock, straightening up, I am the grandson of the cock of Aesculapius, almost as much a god as a master. Your daughter will be very happy with me, in my principality of Coqueliquette, of which you shall have the proof at the first visit you make to our household."

"Blue cock, as blue as litmus, I don't doubt it, but if you were even a little bit human, that wouldn't spoil anything at all."

"Right!" crowed the blue cock. "You're paying attention to that bagatelle? Look at your daughter—she's smiling." At the same time, he took the beautiful Bizibizibizi in his beak by the top of her corset, without her putting up the slightest opposition and flew over the hedge with her.

"Alas, alas," cried Houssihoussa to her husband, through the window, "couldn't you have hit that satanic blue cock on the crest with your spade, and prevented it from carrying off our daughter, the sweet Bizibizibizi?"

But her plaints had no effect, and Brancabanda, shaking his head, said: "Bah! That blue cock is the son of the quasi-divine cock of the god Jetatrape, what could I do? He would have pecked out my eyes, and those of the poor madwoman who doesn't know what she's talking about."

"I don't know what I'm talking about! It's you, you old fool, who doesn't know what you're doing, giving your daughters in marriage to beasts! But you consent because they're your peers! Alas, alas, my poor Bizibizibizi, white as a lily, red as a rose, tender as dew; have I only raised you so delicately for a cock to peck you? Alas, alas, to have a cock or a son-in-law, after having refused so many worthy gentlemen?"

"A quasi-divine cock is worth as much as little pip-squeaks and little apes like Grignotine's sons, whom we refused," said Brancabanda, angrily.[14]

And as he was finishing off his fourth row, he heard the bleating of a sheep, so loudly that it made all the leaves on the trees shake. Brancabanda turned round to see where the bleating was coming from, and at the same time, a beautiful red sheep as big as a bull leapt over the hedge and came toward him, bleating very softly: *bê-hê-hê*.

Brancabanda, who had never seen red sheep, any more than green dogs, yellow wolves or blue cocks, except the ones that the Grignotins had presented, was quite astonished.

"Red sheep, if you are a sheep, what do you want?"

"*Bê-hê-hê*; your servant, Monsieur"—and the sheep made two leaps and a bound; then, launching itself at a walnut-tree, it butted the trunk so hard that all the nuts fell, without a single one remaining. That gave the gar-

---

[14] There is an interruption at this point in the text, in which the listener asks why the narrator keeps repeating things two or three times. He replies that it is a common device among ancient poets, bards and the "illiterate peasants" among whom such tales originate, and suggest that it is akin to the repetition of musical refrains.

dener a good deal of pleasure, for the tree was very tall, and he might have broken his neck beating down the nuts. He called his wife and daughter to pick them up.

Houssihoussa and young Hhouiphhouip, the last of her eight children, ran out quickly. At the garden door, seeing the red sheep, the young woman said to her mother: "My dear Maman, if you want to have a daughter left, go and see what's happening, if you please, for I fear that it's another son-in-law like the others. As for myself, I'll go hide in the house; I'll lock myself in, shoot all the bolts, and barricade the doors."

And the good woman did what her daughter said. She went to her husband and started picking up the walnuts, weeping.

"Wife, where have you left our daughter?"

"Alas, alas, on seeing Monsieur the red sheep, she fled into the house; she's locked herself in, shot the bolts and barricaded the door, for, like her sisters, she doesn't want to be married."

At these words, the red sheep took a run-up at the door of the house and broke it down with a single blow of the head, put the loupinette Hhouiphhouip between its horns as if in an armchair and brought her to her father.

"What are you doing, red sheep?"

"I want this beauty, your youngest daughter, in marriage."

"Beauty…as you say; but it's a great honor for us, again, Monsieur, for I have no doubt that among Messieurs the red sheep you're a very fine gentleman, as the big green dog my son-in-law, who descends from the canine King Opubis, is among the dogs, as the son of the wolf King Limaçon, my son-in-law, is among the wolves, and the great blue cock, descendant of the quasi-divine cock Jetatrape, is among the cocks."

"Monsieur," relied the red sheep, "I descend, in a straight or curved line, from the ram of Phryxus that bore the Golden Fleece; my ancestors once swam over the ocean to establish themselves in Chile in America. I am the king of the Kingdom of Bêhêhê, the land of the red sheep; I will render the beautiful Hhouiphhouip, your daughter, happy and rich, as you will see the first time you visit our household."

"That's all well and good, red sheep, but you wear a fleece. If you were even a little bit human, that wouldn't spoil anything."

"See whether your daughter is discontented!"

"Oh, my poor daughter, you're laughing!" cried Houssihoussa. "That's a bit much!"

But the red sheep, to cut things short and prevent the man and woman from seeing what they ought not to see, said to his wife: "Hold tight, Beauty…"

Hhouiphhouip held on tight to the two horns, and, at the same time, the red sheep leapt over the hedge and disappeared.

Now poor Houssihoussa became desolate again. "Alas, alas, of the four daughters I had, as white as lilies, as red as roses, as tender as dew, I no longer have one, I no longer have any! Carnicroquain, the son of the great Broylesos, Brisecrâne, Massacrotin and Cassechine have eaten my sons, more charming than Renaud, braver than Jean-de-Paris, more valiant than the four sons of Aymon, and perhaps at this moment, a green dog is tearing apart my eldest daughter, a yellow wolf is chewing up my second, a blue cock is pecking my third and a red sheep is browsing my youngest! Alas, alas, how unfortunate I am!"

And Brancabanda, hearing her list all her losses like that, also started weeping and hiding his face; long, deep sighs emerged from the depths of his breast, like those a father makes who is following the coffin of his only son, which is being carried to the tomb. But he pulled himself together eventually, in order to reassure his wife. He said to her: "Houssihoussa, my love, calm down and dry up your tears, for, our daughters having become ugly, what could we have done with them? Now they're well married, and those Messieurs, beasts as they are, seem to me to be quite reasonable, especially Seigneur Red-Sheep, the son of the rich ram Verhus, who carried the gilded fleece."

But the good woman shook her head, did not calm down, and carried on weeping.

Brancabanda and his wife Houssihoussa did not know for a long time how their daughters were—whether they had been torn apart, chewed up, pecked or browsed, or whether they were at ease in their households; for they had not even asked to what country they were going and whether they could write to them. And every day, Houssihoussa said to her husband: "Alas, alas, my poor daughters are dead! If their vile beasts haven't eaten them, they would soon have sent us news. You're the cause of my daughters being lost!"

And the poor fellow replied: "Shut up, woman; it's your pride."

"Isn't a husband the master? If I was foolish, it was necessary to render me sage."

"Ah, that's the truth," said Brancabanda, "but who can vanquish a woman? I'd have done better to have killed you..."

And they argued every day. Brancabanda sustained that his daughters were well, and said so resolutely in front of his wife, in order that she would not deafen him incessantly with her wailing. But when he was all alone, he wept for his four daughters and his four sons.

One day, when Brancabanda was very sad, he went out for a walk; but, seeing that he did not encounter a living soul, he started to weep, saying: "Alas, why wasn't I eaten by the ogres like my sons, or torn apart, chewed up, pecked or browsed like my daughters? Alas, alas, here I am, alone. Who will close my eyes when I'm dead? I no longer have anyone but my wife, and she makes me turn my head away. It is, however, her who rendered me proud and insolent, by telling me every day: 'Are you going to make peasants of our children, and do you want to keep them at the corner of a bush?' Now I'm punished for having listened to her! Oh, if I could just have news of my poor children! Yes, let me have that, and I'll die afterwards, for I no longer have anything to live for now..."

And the poor fellow wept and wept, so much that he could no longer see where he was going, but carried on walking without stopping.

When he had walked for a very long time, he found that he was in a wood, and did not know how to get out of it, for the paths were lost, since no one any longer passed through it in order to get to Charmelieu.

The fellow was very embarrassed, when he saw a beautiful hare in front of him, which had a pink ribbon around its neck. Brancabanda was quite astonished by that encounter, and was even more so when the hare, having perceived him, came straight toward him and spoke to him.

"You must be Monsieur Brancabanda, for no one dares come into these woods any longer because of the ogres who, it's said, have eaten Sacripar, Fandipouf. Farôdor and Craquoman."

"You're right, handsome hare, but it would be better if I'd been eaten by ogres myself than lead the life I'm leading since a green dog tore apart my eldest daughter, a yellow wolf chewed up my second, a blue cock pecked my third and a red sheep browsed my youngest."

"Have you nothing else to say to me, unfortunate fellow?"

"Alas, no, except that I'd like to find the path that will take me home."

"Console yourself; I'll inform you. I'd take you back myself if I had the time, but four hundred paces from here you'll find a white lamb, whom you can ask."

The hare pricked up his ears, leapt up in the air, and started to trot.

When Brancabanda had walked four hundred paces, he heard a little silvery tinkle; he looked round, and saw a pretty lamb, as white as snow, which was browsing.

"Handsome lamb, a Monsieur, a hare by trade, whom I encountered four hundred paces away, had the generosity to tell me that you would do me the honor of informing me as to my route?"

With a soft little bleat, the lamb replied: "You must be Monsieur Brancabanda, for no one dares come into these woods because of the ogres that are said to have eaten Sacripar, Fandipouf, Farôdor and Craquoman?"

"That's right, handsome lamb; but it would be better if I'd been eaten by ogres myself than lead the life I'm leading since a green dog tore apart my eldest daughter, a yellow wolf chewed up my second, a blue cock pecked my third and a red sheep browsed my youngest."

"Have you nothing else to say to me, poor fellow?"

"Alas, no."

"Console yourself and follow your path. Four hundred paces from here, you'll find a white blackbird flying from branch to branch and whistling a little song, whom you should ask."

And Brancabanda walked another four hundred paces; then he heard a chirping voice which trilled:

How charming a cock-husband is,
When he wants to be constant
For a Beauty!
How charming a cock-husband is.
When he wants to be faithful!

Brancabanda raised his head, and perceived in the branches of a bushy beech-tree a blackbird as white as a swan.

"Handsome white blackbird, four hundred paces away I encountered a Monsieur, a lamb by trade, who told me that you could inform me as to my route?"

You must be Monsieur Brancabanda, for no one dares come into these woods because of the ogres that are said to have eaten Sacripar, Fandipouf, Farôdor and Craquoman?"

"Alas, yes, handsome blackbird; but it would be better if I'd been eaten by ogres myself than lead the life I'm leading since a green dog tore apart my eldest daughter, a yellow wolf chewed up my second, a blue cock pecked my third and a red sheep browsed my youngest."

"Have you nothing else to say to me, poor fellow?"

"Alas, no."

"Console yourself and follow your path, for your difficulties will come to an end; four hundred paces from here, you'll find something like a big molehill; a muskrat will come out of it, who will talk to you, but be careful to ask him which way you should go; he's the last one who can tell you."

Somewhat consoled, Brancabanda said to himself: *I only need to know my way in order to get home.* So he walked four hundred paces, through exceedingly dense thickets, and when he came to a clearing he found something like a huge molehill, with a big hole, in front of which there were nutshells, the cups of acorns and crushed ears of wheat.

As the fellow was wondering whether that was really the place that the white blackbird had indicated to him, a pretty rat emerged from the hole, the most beautiful yellow in color, with orange feet and ears, a blue muzzle and a green beard, which reeked of musk, like a fop.

"Handsome rat, four hundred paces away I encountered a Monsieur, a white blackbird by trade, as you are a musk-rat, who told me that you could inform me as to my route to return home, to my poor wife Houssihoussa, who must be quite desolate...?"

The yellow-red-blue-green muskrat started guioring,[15] laughing with all its might.

"You must be Monsieur Brancabanda, for no one dares come into these woods because of the ogres that are said to have eaten Sacripar, Fandipouf, Farôdor and Craquoman?"

"You're right, handsome yellow-red-blue-green muskrat; but it would be better for me if I'd been eaten

---

[15] Author's note, credited to the narrator: "Squealing like a rat—whence comes the word *guiorante*, meaning a shrill voice." I have transposed the French term rather than substituting "squeaking," which does not give the right impression.

by ogres myself than lead the life I'm leading since a green dog tore apart my eldest daughter, a yellow wolf chewed up my second, a blue cock pecked my third and a red sheep browsed my youngest..."

"Follow me, Monsieur," said the muskrat. "I'll take you to within four hundred paces of your dwelling, but if you had asked me to take you somewhere else, I would have taken you there."

"Monseigneur Yellow-red-blue-green Muskrat, could you have taken me to where my daughters are?"

"I'm not a Monseigneur, but one of the commensals of the beautiful Queen Hhouiphhouip, your youngest daughter, the wife of His Two-Horned[16] Majesty King Bêhêhê, the sublime and excellent monarch of the Red Sheep."

"Handsome rat, what are you telling me? My poor Hhouiphhouip hasn't been browsed by His Two-Horned Majesty King Bêhêhê, and she isn't dead?"

"Patata, dead! But as for browsed, that's something else. It's not permitted for me to tell you more. Let's return to your home, where Madame Houssihoussa is very chagrined, and when your heart bids you, come back and find me, following the same route you took to go astray—for it's getting dark and you'd never recognize the path we're about to take, which is the shortest."

Brancabanda followed the yellow-red-blue-green muskrat, which took him to four hundred paces from his home, where the poor fellow, very weary and dying of hunger, found the good Houssihoussa, his wife, half dead of the fear she had of ghosts.

---

[16] The word *biscornu* [two-horned] is rarely used literally in French, but almost always figuratively, to refer to something misshapen or oddly composed.

Brancabanda told her everything that had happened to him, and the good Houssihoussa was overjoyed to have news of her dear Hhouiphhouip—which occupied her so much that she dreamed about her all night, as well as her other daughters.

It seemed to her that she saw Hhûeip, her eldest, in an ivory castle, more beautiful and radiant than she had ever been. Hhûhhuip, her second, was in an ebony palace, full of riches, and she was so very beautiful that it was an admiration. Bizibizibizi was in a beautiful coop of golden wire as large as the Red House, seated on trees as large and high as the steeple of Nitry, where there were iron teeth to climb up to it. As for Hhouiphhoiuip, she saw her in a crystal palace covered in rubies, served by pretty green monkeys.

But what worried her, in her dream, was that nothing was served on her eldest daughter's table but carcasses, for which her husband went to search in ditches. On that of her second daughter were sheep, all raw and bloody. On that of the third there were worms and other trivia, with something even worse. Finally, on the table of the youngest, there was straw, hay, bran, walnut-leaves, etc.

When she woke up, she said: "My daughters are well lodged, but my God, they're very poorly nourished!"

Immediately, she told her husband what she had dreamed, who said to her: "It's all right; it's only a dream."

The next morning, as soon as it was light, they got up. Houssihoussa made a good breakfast for her husband so that he could return very quickly to look for their daughters, and when he had eaten well, she filled his pockets with more; and he set forth.

At first, Brancabanda followed, or thought he was following, the previous day's route, but he walked all day without finding the hare with the pink collar, the white lamb with the silvery bell, the white black bird or the yellow-red-blue-green muskrat with the shrill laugh, and because he wanted to go astray he could never reach a destination. He went home at nightfall, chagrinned and very weary, to tell his wife about his bad luck.

For the first time in her life, poor Houssihoussa gave him some good advice. "Perhaps, my husband, we took to many precautions? If you want to succeed, it's necessary to set forth without thinking about anything and abandon yourself to hazard, for the fay Ouroucoucou and the genii like that; and when one is very, very weary and no longer knows in which direction to go, they come to your aid..."

Brancabanda told himself that she was right, also for the first time in his life; with the result that they embraced, very glad to find such good accord for their old age.

The fellow remained at home for several months in succession, cultivating his garden, not wanting to set forth until he was thinking about nothing at all—but he was always thinking about something, sometimes his daughters, sometimes his sons, and sometimes his wife, who was no longer half as shrewish, which made him think that he was living in paradise. He spent a good six months without being able to say to himself that he was not thinking about anything—which, in our day, would be reckoned a great prodigy.

Finally, one morning, when he was all I-don't-know-what, he took it into his head to read a book of those days, written by a little gnome of the Black Forest, entitled *Les Mille-et-une fadaises*;[17] and he had hardly read two pages when he found himself thinking about nothing at all, to such an extent that, feeling weighed down, he took his staff and went out in order to clear his head.

A few nonsensical things passed through his mind, but they were so destitute of common sense that they counted for nothing, and he walked mechanically for a long, long way, and would have gone even further if he had not felt hunger, having had no dinner. Mechanically, therefore, he turned round and tried to retrace his steps. Once again, he marched for a long, long time, until, collapsing with weariness, he sat down at the foot of a tree.

He had no sooner sat down than he heard leaping and gamboling around him in the foliage. He turned round heavily, for he still had the two pages of nonsense from his book in his head, and he saw the handsome hare with the pink collar, as before.

That reinvigorated him immediately.

"Handsome hare, have pity on me and inform me of my way..." He did not add anything more.

The hare with the pink collar sent him to the white lamb with the silvery bell; the lamb with the silvery bell sent him to the white blackbird; and the white blackbird sent him to the yellow-red-blue-green-muskrat.

---

[17] *Les Mille et une fadaises* (1742; tr. as *A Thousand and One Follies*) is an extended *conte bleu* by Jacques Cazotte. Restif and Cazotte became close friends when they met in Fanny de Beauharnais; salon in the late 1780s, but Restif was not personally acquainted with him when he made this slightly odd remark.

When the yellow-red-blue-green muskrat saw him, it started laughing and guioring even louder than the first time.

"I'm charmed to see you again," he guiored. "Tell me now, then, Monsieur Brancabanda, husband of the good Houssihoussa, father of the beautiful Queen Hhouiphhouip, spouse of His Two-Horned Majesty King Bêhêhê, the most handsome of the red sheep; of the beautiful Bizibizibizi, wife of His Crested Eminence Cocodinq, Prince of the blue cocks; the beautiful Hhûhhuip, wife of His Crunching Highness the terrible Hihouhâh, Duc of the yellow wolves; and the beautiful Hhûeip, wife of His Mordant Highness the nimble Ouapouahoup, Marquis of the green dogs, where do you want to go?"

Brancabanda, to whom that enumeration gave pause for thought, replied swiftly: "To my daughters' homes."

"Which one?"

"Hhûeip, wife of the nimble Ouapouahoup, Marquis of the green dogs, my eldest daughter."

"In that case," said the yellow-red-blue-green muskrat, "go back the way you've just come, to where you found the hare with the pink collar. He's the favorite of the beautiful Marquise Hhûeip, wife of His Mordant Highness Monseigneur Ouapouahoup, the nimblest of the Green Dogs."

The fellow was very annoyed at having to retrace his steps, because he was very weary and he was dying of hunger, but the yellow-red-blue-green muskrat had already gone back into his molehill and there was no means of talking to him again. So he returned to the white blackbird, who sent him to the white lamb with the silvery bell, who accompanied him to the beautiful hare with the pink collar.

"Handsome hare, a Monsieur, a muskrat by trade, told me to address myself to you in order find the dwelling of my dear Hhûeip, my eldest daughter, the wife of my son-in-law Monseigneur His Mordant Highness the Marquis Ouapouahoup, the nimblest of the Green Dogs.

"Yes, Monsieur," replied the hare in the pink collar, and I would have taken you there the first time I saw you if you had asked; but we are like judges, we cannot grant anything beyond what is asked of us. Follow me."

The hare with the pink collar took Brancabanda along a comfortable little path, where he found a pretty ivory chariot hitched to twelve beautiful roe deer, in which he sat, and the hare with the pink collar climbed up to the driver's seat. Immediately, the twelve roe deer started running so forcefully that they went as fast as the wind.

When they had run for a long, long way they arrived in a plain in the middle of which stood a superb ivory castle with columns of the Doric order, the grooves of which were silvered and the capitals solid silver.

At the great gate of the courtyard there was a huge cat whose whiskers were a good two ells long, with a superb baldric—for he was Swiss by nation[18]—who said: "I'm here, although it's necessary to open the door without asking who it is..."

The chariot went in as far as the third courtyard, where Brancabanda saw a great many hares and rabbits, and well-harnessed roe deer. He had no sooner got down from the chariot than a beautiful Lady, covered in pearls, who had come running when she heard the noise, supported by four doe-hares, her chambermaids, came to-

---

[18] In France, doormen are known as "Suisse" [Swiss], so this is a joke of sorts.

ward him with open arms, exclaiming; "Oh, it's my dear father!"

He recognized her by her voice and the bounding of his heart as his dear Hhûeip, his eldest daughter, and he almost collapsed with pleasure on seeing her more beautiful than she had ever been.

"Bonjour, my dear daughter! How are you? Are you happy? Oh, my daughter, my poor daughter, is it really you? How are you?" And he said the same things over and over while his daughter embraced him, and did not even give her the time to reply, for his hands were trembling, his tongue was stammering, his eyes were streaming, his heart was melting and he did not feel at ease.

Finally, in a moment when the fellow was contemplating his daughter, mute with ecstasy, she replied to him:

"As you see, my dear Father, I have everything I could wish for. And my good Mother?"

"Oh, if only she were here, if only she were here! And your husband?"

"He's out, Father, on the ditches, where he's looking for a carcass for our supper."

"Oh, my dear daughter, what are you saying?"

"The truth," relied Hhûeip, laughing. "You'll have the proof of it shortly, and you'll agree, my dear Father, that I'm very fortunate."

"I'm very hungry, but I assure you that I shan't eat a morsel in your house unless one of those hares or rabbits is killed for me and put on the spit."

"Oh, my dear Father, what are you thinking! Kill our servants and eat them! Are we ogres?"

Brancabanda was ashamed of his incongruity. He was about to make his apologies to his daughter's domestic staff when he heard a canine voice, much more powerful than that of the largest bulldog.

"Ah, there's my husband!" said the beautiful Hhûeip, jumping with joy—and she ran to meet him, shouting: "Toutou, Toutoutou! Chiou! Chiou! My father has come! My father has come! Have you had a good find? Oh, what a lovely carcass; it's a carthorse at least."

"Oupoup!"—that is the "parbleu" of dogs of all colors—"May he be welcome! There's enough for a feast." To his hunting-cats and kitchen-cats, he said: "Arrange that, all of you."

Brancabanda advanced toward His Mordant Highness the nimble Ouapouahoup, Marquis of the Green Dogs, but when he saw the carcass, he turned his head away and pinched his nose.

"Oupoup! Good evening, Father!"

"Good evening, Son-in-law."

"Are you well, and our good Mother?"

"As to that, my Son-in-law, we've had a great deal of chagrin, and my poor wife is in very poor health."

"I'll give you a restorative for her."

"I'll be much obliged to you...but can you not, my son-in-law the Marquis, give me a little now for myself, for I'm collapsing with weakness.

"Oupoup! Right away, Father; it will be done in a minute."

Ouapouahoup, the nimblest of dogs, who had conserved his old mores, immediately started cooking himself, as Achilles once did, breaking, carving and tearing with his teeth and throwing pieces as he went into a large cooking-pot on a huge fire.

What a marvel! The more the bones boiled, the more flesh there was, and they had not been boiling for a quarter of an hour when a delicious odor spread all around, compared with which the perfume of the most exquisite stews is nothing but a stink. And Brancabanda, whom hunger had rendered a trifle sad, began to feel his heart expanding, and said to himself: *Well, well, what's this? My daughter Madame la Marquise of the Green Dogs might not have as much to complain about as I had imagined...*

As everyone lent a hand, the supper was soon ready. They sat down at table. A she-cat in an apron as white as snow took from the cooking-pot an excellent clear soup, which the beautiful Hhûeip had her father taste in a sculpted silver spoon. Brancabanda found it delicious, and, which pleased him even more, he recovered all his strength without his appetite being diminished.

"Well, Father," said His Mordant Highness the Marquis of the Green Dogs, what would you like me to serve you on your plate now? You have only to imagine it, for the dishes I shall serve you will have in your mouth whatever taste and whatever sauce you wish."

The fellow, who was hungry, did not want very delicate things; he wanted a nice meaty turkey-leg, with a remoulade underneath. He had no sooner put a piece in his mouth than he found the turkey so exquisite in its taste that he set about eating for four.

"Well, let's drink, Father," said Ouapouahoup. "And immediately, the hare wine-waiter served, in beautiful rock-crystal glasses with silver flowers, the water in which the carcass had been boiled. On seeing that, Brancabanda started to say that he was not thirsty, but an ambrosial odor spread over the table, which made him want to taste the liquid—and as soon as he had placed his lips on the edge of the glass, he drained it dry, so exquisite did he find the beverage. He presented his cup three times in succession and emptied it without leaving a drop, although it held a pint, Flavigny measure, which is large enough for a child to hide behind.

When he had eaten and drank his fill, the beautiful Hhûeip, accompanied by the hare in the pink collar, took her gather into an ivory chamber where there was a beautiful bed with a mattress of Icelandic eiderdown, ivory armchairs with cushions in which one could sink to the ears, and rock-crystal vases with silver floral designs, into which flowers with a perfume that surpassed roses had been placed.

Her Serene Highness the beautiful Hhûeip, Marquise of the Green Dogs, kissed him, wished him good night and withdrew in order to go to bed, leaving the hare with the pink collar behind in order to sleep at his feet and chase away the flies and gnats, if any came in.

Brancabanda, who was very tired, and who had drunk like a Templar, slept without waking until it was broad daylight.

When his sleep had dissipated he wanted to get up, and searched for his clothes, but instead of the ones he had taken off when he went to bed, he found fine amber-perfumed underwear, a superb coat in the Spanish style, a blond wig as big as a barrel, a hat with a superb plume, red silk stockings and shoes with pointed toes.

"That's for you," said he hare with the pink collar. "I'll leave you, and go where my duty summons me."

He got dressed, therefore, after a Turkish-bath-hare had cut his hair and turned up his moustache. His adornment changed him so much that, in passing along the gallery to go to the apartment of Her Serene Highness the Marquise, his daughter, he perceived himself in beautiful Coqueliquette mirrors—which are far more beautiful than those from Venice—and did not recognize himself, which often happens to people in similar situations, for he mistook himself for a Spanish grandee. He bowed profoundly, taking off his plumed hat; and, seeing that the Spanish grandee returned his salute in the same fashion, he became confused and went down on his knees. The Spanish grandee did the same.

"Come on, Monseigneur," Brancabanda said to him. "You're making fun of your servant!" He saw the Spanish grandee's lips moving, but could not hear his words, and thought he was telling him to get up and pass on—so he stood up, and saw with pleasure that the Spanish grandee got up with him. He bowed again, ready to pass on; but, seeing that the Spanish grandee was going the same way, he wanted to let him go first. Great debates followed between the Spanish grandee and the Father off Her Serene Highness the Marquise, mistress of the palace

It seemed to Brancabanda that he heard the other say to him: "No, Monsieur, I'm a Spanish grandee it's true, and in that quality, more than all the Kings and Princes on Earth, but you're in the home of Madame your daughter."

To that the fellow responded with respectful representations. That might have gone on all day if two hare pages had not seen him and, after having amused themselves like pages, imitating his reverences behind his back, had gone to tell their mistress how much polite respect Monsieur Brancabanda, her father, had for himself. The beautiful Hhûeip came to find him, laughing like a madwoman—not that she was making fun of her father; she was too respectful for that, but she made a meal out of amusing him with his error.

"Papa," she said, embracing him, "forgive my inattention; I should have come to look for you in your room, or at least warned you what you that what you see there is a glass that reflects things; it's yourself that you can see, and my image that appears next to yours."

Brancabanda, who had never seen a mirror and was unfamiliar with their effect, smiled at his daughter's speech. "Still the same, my child," he said. That's how you took pleasure in your childhood, playing tricks on your sisters and your poor brothers..."—at the words *your poor brothers*, tears came into his eyes—"...and sometimes on us. Come on, I'm glad that you still have things to make you laugh, and that marriage hasn't taken away all your playfulness, for it's sometimes pleasurable..."

The beautiful Hhûeip did not want to contradict her father, even with reason, and her father's tears, the memory of her brothers, her sisters, and her poor mother having swollen her heart, she shed two beautiful tears as big as pearls, and took her father by the hand.

Brancabanda followed his daughter into a large and rich apartment, all in ivory, where a fine breakfast was served. When they had eaten and supped well, Ouapoahoup said:

"Well, Father, you can see now what the fate of your eldest daughter is. Have you any complaint?"

"Oh, my Son-in-law the Marquis of the Green Dogs, it is, on the contrary, very fine, and another time I won't be so quick to judge things about which I know nothing. But tell me, where are your children?"

"Oh, my Father, my dear Father," said the green dog, with tears in his eyes, "If you knew me...but that cannot be, as yet; only know, in the meantime, that when loyalty and fidelity quit human beings, they took refuge among us, and I shall prove that to you by my attachment to my dear wife and my respect for you and my Mother."

"Oh, the fine fellow!" said Brancabanda, moved. "Is it possible that he's a dog?"

"You saw yesterday, my Father," His Mordant Highness the Marquis Ouapouahoup went on, "how I can extract excellent nourishment from vile filth, and you regret that I'm a dog! But that's not all; would you like to see the bones now? My dear wife, show your manufacture to your Father."

"I'd like that," said Brancabanda, "Provided that it doesn't delay me, for I'm in haste to see my poor wife; it seems to me that I can only enjoy my daughter's happiness by half while Houssihoussa doesn't know about it."

Immediately, the beautiful Hhûeip opened an ivory door and Brancabanda saw hares in white leather aprons, who were turning pieces of ivory on lathes, in order to make all kinds of objects of them.

"This is how I make use of the bones," she said.

Brancabanda embraced his daughter, transported by joy.

"Oh, how I'm looking forward to telling that to your mother, my poor Houssihoussa! Let's go, I need to get back."

"It's more than a hundred leagues away," replied Ouapouahoup, "But you'll arrive this evening. And in order that you can come back whenever you wish, or go to the homes of your others son-in-law, here's an ivory talisman. I'm the only one of my brothers-in-law who has one, so look after it carefully. Every time you want to go to see one or other of your daughters, tap with it on the threshold of your door and say: 'By the nose of my son-in-law the Green Dog, let his chariot, his hare coachman and his roe deer come here'—and they'll be there right away. If you want to go to the home of my other brothers-in-law, you say of the yellow wolf, 'by the teeth,' of the blue cock, 'by the crest,' and of the red sheep, 'by the horns,' and immediately, each of them will harness his chariot, as he'll have heard you, and will send it to your door. But you must always come alone; your wife will never be able to accompany you, as long as the dog barks, the wolf howls, the cock crows and the sheep bleats."

After saying that, the Green Dog grandee had provisions loaded on to the chariot that was to take his father-in-law home, and restoratives for the good Houssihoussa, with pretty objects in ivory. Hhûeip and he embraced Brancabanda. Then they each blew blast on a whistle made from a pieced apricot stone, in order to summon the coachman hare with the pink collar.

As soon as he was in his seat, the fellow climbed into the chariot and sat down, blessing the Heaven that had given his eldest daughter in marriage to such an honest dog. And he said to himself: *Oh, if my other daughters are only half as happy as the couple here, I'll have nothing more for which to wish!*

In the meantime, the chariot and the twelve roe deer where whizzing like the wind, traveling a dozen leagues an hour, with the result that at eight o'clock in the evening, they arrived at Brancabanda's door. The fellow got down and the roe deer unloaded the presents, before returning as fast as they had come, guided by the hare with the pink collar.

"Houssihoussa, my poor wife, open the door to your husband, who has come back from more than a hundred leagues away!"

Houssihoussa had no sooner heard her husband's voice than she cried: "Is that you, Brancabanda?"

"Yes, yes, it's me., who has come back from seeing our son-in-law, His Mordant Highness Oupouahoup, descendant of Opubis, Marquis of the Green Dogs and our daughter Her Serene Highness Hhûeip, who has become even more beautiful than before, and who really is a Marquise.

Hearing that, the good woman came to open the door exclaiming: "It would be better to be a milkmaid among humans than a Marquise among dogs."

Seeing her husband with a fine plume on his head, with a beautiful coat, lovely red silk stockings and the rest, she curtsied, saying: "Where is my husband, Monseigneur?"

Brancabanda started laughing, and laughing, exclaiming "You said it! I'm your seigneur!" And he embraced her.

When the good woman saw the pretty presents in ivory with silver floral designs that her son-in-law the green dog and her daughter Hhûeip had send her, she wept with joy, saying: "Oh my poor daughter! Has she kept any for herself?"

"That's not all, Wife; here's a little specimen of the cuisine that our son-in-law, His Mordant Highness the Green Dog, makes for his wife, Her Serene Highness our poor Hhûeip, for whom we have wept so much; set out the tablecloth and let's eat; your dream was true, but it didn't tell you everything..."

Houssihoussa set out the tablecloth, and Brancabanda laid the table with all sorts of dishes.

"Oh, my Wife, what would you like to eat?"

The good woman asked for the things she liked best, and her husband served them. "Here they are..." And they were—which rendered the good woman very content.

Then her husband told her every detail of what he had seen: how their son-in-law His Mordant Highness of the Green Dogs made excellent stews with carcasses, and beautiful ivory with the bones; how he had an ivory palace, in which there were exceedingly polite Spanish grandees; how he had hares for lackeys, cats for cooks, rabbits for cleaners and roe deer for horses; and how one drank carcass-water that was better than all the wines in the world.

Then they drank a good cup, and went to bed.

Brancabanda and his wife lived for more than a week on the provisions he had brought; and the soup, of which they took a few spoonfuls every day, rendered them all their strength, so completely that they would never have been so happy if they had not thought about their sons, which wrung their hearts.

When they saw that they only had enough for another two or three days, Brancabanda said to his wife: "I know what it's necessary to do: to go and see my other daughters; and I give you notice that I'll be sleeping tonight in the house of our poor Hhûhhuip, the spouse of the treble Hihouhâh, Duc of Wolfville, the capital of the yellow wolves."

Immediately, he took out his ivory talisman, and then he tapped it on the threshold of the door, saying: "By the tooth of my son-in-law His Crunching Highness the Yellow Wolf, let his chariot come here, harnessed as he intends..."

He had no sooner pronounced those words than a beautiful ebony and silver chariot arrived at the door, with the white lamb with the tinkling bell for a coachman, and a dozen four-horned white sheep for horses.

Houssihoussa was very content, and started so say: "I'll go with you, my husband..."—which caused the white lamb with the tinkling bell to bleat dolorously and shake its head negatively.

"Alas," said Brancabanda, "that can't be; my son-in-law the green dog forbade it, for as long as dogs bark, wolves howl, cocks row and sheep bleat."

There was no response to make to such a good reason, so Houssihoussa, although she was very argumentative, made none. And the fellow bid his wife adieu and departed.

The white sheep went like the wind, but still took ten hours to go from Brancabanda's house to that of His Crunching Highness Hihouhâh, Duc of the Yellow Wolves, who had married the beautiful Hhûhhuip.

Finally, at about ten o'clock in the evening, the chariot arrived in a gorge between high mountains covered in woods, and on the pinnacle of a rock Brancabanda perceived a beautiful castle of ebony, of the Ionic order, the columns and pilasters of which had capitals of rock crystal with golden threads and beautiful gilded grooves.

At the door there was a huge ram with eight horns, with a halberd and a baldric—for he was Swiss by nation—and a large carbuncle in the middle of his forehead, which His Crunching Highness Hihouhâh had been clever enough to steal from a dragon-fay.

Dragons, whether fays or not, are in the habit, when they want to drink, of removing their carbuncle from their throat and putting it in the edge of the stream to provide illumination while they drink, and the dragon-fay had put its own on the edge of a nectar-spring, which emerged at that time from the pierced rock on the peak of Tenerife in the Canary Islands, from which canaries come. His Highness Hihuouhâh, Duc of Wolves, saw it, took it and destined it to ornament the forehead of the great Rakiakiakiâh, his doorman; the carbuncle weighted a good ten pounds and was so brilliant that it replaced the Sun when it had set and illuminated the whole castle and its surroundings for several leagues around—with the consequence that even though it was night when Brancabanda, the lamb with the silvery bell and the twelve white sheep arrived in Wolfville, the capital of the Yellow Wolves, the fellow thought that it was still day-time.

As soon as the beautiful Hhûhhuip, Brancabanda's second daughter and the wife of His Crunching Highness Hihouhâh, Duc of the Yellow Wolves, heard the noise of the chariot she ran to the door of the castle, supported by four white ewes, her chambermaids, and ordered Rahkiakiakiâh to open the door.

"I can see that it's your father, Madame," replied the doorman.

"Oh, it's my dear Papa!" said the Duchesse of the Wolves, throwing herself into Brancabanda's arms.

The fellow recognize her by her voice as his dear Hhûhhuip, for she was so ornamented and covered with emeralds mingled with topazes, beryls and chrysolites, that she dazzled him. Even her ewes had sapphire necklaces and chrysoprase rings on their ankles.

"Oh, my daughter, my dear Hhûhhuip, it's you, and more beautiful than you've ever been! How are you? Are you as happy as our elder sister? It's you, my daughter, it's you...it's you...and here you are, as you were before...before..."

His daughter embraced him without replying, for her poor heart was melting with the pleasure of feeling herself clasped in the arms of her poor father, who had loved her so much.

Finally, she opened her mouth, and her first words were: "And my dear Mother, how is she?"

"Well, very well, since we've had news of your sister Hhûeip, who is living happily with her husband, His Mordant Highness the Marquis, the nimblest of the dogs, although, in truth, he's bulkier than the biggest bulldog. And you, how are you finding it in your household?"

"You can see, my dear Father, that I have everything I wish."

"And your husband, where is he?"

"He's down there at a corner of the wood, lying in wait for a sheep for our supper."

"What, my daughter! Being as rich as you appear to be, what need does he have to be lurking there like a thief?"

"You can't think so, my dear Papa! He's making war, and that's one of his rights as a sovereign; what is called stealing for the rabble is, for them, called making conquests, and what is called cowardly murder in the common people is called victory for them, which is the most beautiful word, one scholar says, in all the languages spoken by humans, green dogs, yellow wolves, blue cocks and red sheep."

The fellow had no reply to that; in any case, he was very glad to see his daughter taking her husband's part, which every sage wife should always do on every occasion. He took care not to say anything, as he had in the home of his son-in-law the green dog, about them putting a liveried lamb on the spit for his meal—besides which, he was not as tired and not as hungry.

He therefore amused himself, while waiting for his son-in-law, in seeing his daughter's apartments, where there were beautiful paintings representing the finest actions of the wolves: their cunning, their audacity and the heroism of some of the great wolves, who had even tried to achieve the submission of the human species, such as the Beast of Gevaudan, which, greater than Alexander, attacked an entire province single-handed and desolated it, so that he was regarded more as a god than a wolf. There were also traces of humanity, although very ancient, such as those of the she-wolf, one of the ancestors of His Crunching Highness Hehouhâh, more humane than Amulius, the King of Alba Longa, who had suckled the twins Remus and Romulus, who had been exposed for ferocious beasts, etc., etc.

While Brancabanda, conducted by his daughter, was taking a great deal of pleasure in that, he heard a howl that made him tremble, and all the servants, even the ram with eight horns, which, without thinking about it, hid his head, thus causing a carbuncular eclipse in the palace and for ten leagues around, which puzzled scholars greatly—but he soon recovered his courage.

"Ah, there's my husband," said Her Serene Highness Duchesse Hhûhhuip, and she immediately ran to meet him, shouting: "My Father has come! My Father has come! My dear Hihouhâh, did the little war go well? Oh, what a beautiful Flemish sheep!"

"Hahoûh!"—that is the "parbleu" of wolves—"May he be welcome! Here's something to regale him, for I've also killed a Prussian deer and an English boar, which my soldiers are bringing in my chariot."

In the meantime, Brancabanda, who was not yet very assured, so frightened had he been, advanced very quietly, thinking: *The appearances of the cuisine are better here than in the home of my son-in-law the dog.*

"Hahoûh! Bonsoir, my Father!"

"Bonsoir, my Son-in-law!"

"Are you well, my Father, as well as our good Mother, your wife?"

"Well, enough, my Son, since I've seen your brother-in-law, my son-in-law the green dog, and my eldest daughter, your sister-in-law, from whom I obtained the piece of ivory that enables me to summon your chariot and those of the others I want to see. My poor wife was in poor health, but my son-in-law the green dog gave me a restorative for her, which made her feel much better, and me too."

"Good! That's nothing! I'll give you a jelly that will rejuvenate her by twenty years and make all her teeth grow back."

"Oh, I'll be much obliged to you! Can't you, at present, let me have a little for myself, for I'm missing twenty-two, and I'd sup with a better appetite!"

"Hahoûh—right away, Father, it'll be done in a minute."

His Crunching Highness the Great Yellow Wolf immediately set about skinning the sheep, and the deer, which he had his six cooks butcher, as well as the boar. Then it was served, raw, on the table, following the practice of Messieurs the wolves of all colors, who have not abandoned their ancient customs.

Brancabanda was quite surprised, especially on seeing the white lamb, his coachman, eating with the wolves. He said to himself: Ah! *There's the hitch! It's that everyone eats raw meat here. I'm going to get thin...* He was already beginning to pull a face, when his son-in-law His Crunching Highness the Great Hihhouhâh perceived it.

"My dear Father," he said, "I could prove to you by good arguments and experience that you're wrong to

147

have any repugnance about eating raw meat, but I think it much more respectful on my part to do what you appear to desire; if anyone ought to yield in your children's home, it isn't you, even if they were a hundred times right..."

As soon as it was said it was done; he great Hihouhâh filleted all the meat properly, as Achilles once did, and threw the pieces into great silver cauldrons, with the exception of a few morsels that the fox cooks put on the spit, which was turned by very pretty violet dogs. As for the bones, they were put in a platinum pot, which was covered with a well-sealed lid.

"Well," said the Great Yellow Wolf, "I'll cook all that for you without fire; one of my old foxes, a skillful physicist, has made, large liquid lens, more perfect than the one in the Infanta's garden,[19] with which one collects the rays of my ram doorman's carbuncle and directs them at the cauldrons, bring them to the boil, and on to the spits, in order to roast."

Brancabanda was amazed by everything the Great Hihouhâh said, and what was even more surprising was that the meat was cooked in less than five minutes. But it was necessary to smell the fine odor that all of it exhaled! It was so delicious that the fellow would have

---

[19] The largest lens ever made when the present story was written, devised by Jean-Charles Trudaine de Montigny and constructed by Claude de Bernières on behalf of the Académie des Sciences, was composed of two hemispherical pieces of glass fused at the edges, containing thirty-five gallons of liquid. It was placed in the "Infanta's garden" then adjacent to the Louvre in 1774, and functioned as a burning glass with the aid of a maller lens.

been almost content, if it had not awakened his appetite too forcefully.

When everything was ready, His Crunching Highness the Great Yellow Wolf had it served; and the part that was to be sent as a present to the good Houssihoussa, his mother-in-law, was immediately put to one side. Before eating, however, the Great Wolf opened the sealed platinum pot and showed Brancabanda all the bones reduced to marmalade. He put half a spoonful into his mouth, and immediately—an admirable thing!—all his teeth grew back, with the consequence that he got ready to make full use of his jaws.

"Well, my Father," said the Great Yellow Wolf, "What would you like to eat now? You only have to imagine it, for I can treat you even better than my brother-in-law the green dog.

Brancabanda wished for all the things he liked best, even poultry, and found it all before him, with the taste he desired, but so delicious that, having all his teeth, he set out to devour it rather than eat it.

"Let's drink, Father," said Hehougâh, then. At the same time, two snow-white lambs appeared, each with a beautiful rock crystal vase on its back bordered with glen flowers, and pissed into them until they were full.

Hey hey hey! the guest thought to himself, *everything was beginning to go too well for there not to be something else a trifle singular to expect! But I'll say that I only drink water...*

While he was muttering that, the filled cups were placed on the table, where they exhaled an odor compared to which the carcass-water was nothing. Brancabanda tried a sip, but he found the beverage so good that he swallowed it all in a single draught, and presented his glass—which was even larger than the one in the home of his son-in-law the green dog—to be re-filled.

A young ewe, even whiter and more delicate than the first, immediately poured her topaz liquor into it, clearer that a rock pool; the fellow drank, presented the vessel again; drank again; a presented it again, so many times that a hundred young ewes, each more beautiful than the last, were scarcely enough to slake his thirst. Finally, however, he was sated.

When he had eaten as well as he had drunk, the Her beautiful Highness Hhûhhuip, followed by the white lamb, took her father personally to a chamber of jet, ornamented by mirrors and paintings, the frames of which were sculpted gold. She had the ewe chambermaids undress him and put him in a bed of the finest down of large Greenland ducks, where he slept without waking until it as broad daylight, with the white lamb lying at his feet.

When he woke up in the morning, Brancabanda found, laid out on a crimson velvet armchair, a beautiful puce coat in the French style, braided with gold, with a plumed hat, white silk stockings, fine leather shoes with red heels and gemmed buckles that covered the whole foot, a beautiful épée with a damascened steel hilt enriched with topazes and emeralds, with a beautiful shirt decorated in Alençon needlepoint.

"That's for you," the white lamb told him, "but I'm going where my duty summons me..."

As he dressed, he thought about what had happened to him in the house of his son-in-law the green dog, with the Spanish grandee, and promised himself not to pay any attention to a Grand Duc and peer of France if he found one disputing his passage—but it is necessary not to swear to anything.

When he was ready he went out, without having looked at himself in the mirrors in the bedroom, over which Her Highness the Duchesse Hhûhhuip had pulled a green curtain, for fear that their glare in the first rays of the sun might dazzle her dear father. In the gallery, however, garnished with faceted mirrors like multipliers, he saw with surprise a host of young Frenchmen who all resembled one another, just like the young men of today, all walking slowly looking from side to side, as if in quest of admiration.

This time, he thought, *my daughter Hhûhhuip isn't going to tell me, like her elder sister, that that's me, even though their clothes resemble mine! I'm not so young, nor so handsome, nor so conceited, nor so impolite...*

As he said that, in order not to resemble them, he started saluting them. Immediately, all the hats were raised and all the backs inclined, as if they were all moved by the same brass wore. Content with the promptitude with which the young men returned his salute, the fellow changed his opinion of them, saying: *Perhaps the youth of today is better than that of my time, which had no respect for age, and I judged them too hastily...*

Unfortunately, a few paces further on, he took it into his head to spit, and at the same time, all those well-disciplined young men started spitting in his face. He put up his hand, and, not feeling anything, was very surprised; but what shocked him was that all the young men started mimicking him, also putting their hands to their faces with a vexed expression. Brancabanda felt a surge of petulance, such as he had not experienced for thirty years.

"Scoundrels!" he cried, putting his hand on the hilt to his sword.

Scoundrel, repeated the young men, from one end of the room to the other, all simultaneously putting their hands on the hilts of their épées.

"What can you do," said Brancabanda, sighing, "one poor old man against a vigorous army of young insolents?"

Insolent!

He took his hand off his sword, even though he had been called insolent in the home of Her Highness Hhûhhuip, Duchesse of the Yellow Wolves, his second daughter. His moderation was imitated by the entire company.

Two young ewes—two of those who had slaked his thirst so well the previous evening—perceived him gesticulating and ran, laughing, to inform their mistress that Seigneur Brancabanda was fencing in the gallery. Her Highness the beautiful Hhûhhuip came to meet her father in order to embrace him. The worthy man was furious.

"What's the matter, Papa?" she asked.

"I demand justice Madame, for the insults I've received in your house from this troop of ill-bred..."

Ill-bred.

"Where are they, Papa?"

Alas, far from seeing a troop there, there was not a single one.

"You didn't see them, then?"

"No."

"Would you believe that they mocked me, spat in my face, and were all ready to draw their swords simultaneously against a poor old men?"

Poor old man.

In spite of her respect for her father, Her Serene Highness the beautiful Hhûhhuip uttered a loud burst of laughter, which was repeated by four or five hundred young women as beautiful as the day, mingled with the young Frenchmen.

"What, my daughter! You and your retinue are joining in with them?"

"No, Father—it's you whose image you can see. They're Coqueliquette mirrors, shaped and posed in such a fashion that they multiply objects."

"Get away! I see a young coxcomb, do I not? You're just like your sister Her Serene Highness the Marquise of Dogs, but this is even less credible."

"Listen to me, Papa! The jelly of the bones of Flemish sheep, Prussian deer and English boar that you ate yesterday and enabled you to recover all your teeth has rejuvenated you as you are there. Don't you see that I'm repeated as many times as you?"

"Patata! They're your followers! Don't I know that a Highness has as many as that? And then, they spoke to me."

"That's the echo."

"Let's leave it there," said Brancabanda, embracing his daughter. "You're a good sovereign, and I'm not annoyed that you're excusing your subjects. I believe, however, that I'm young, but I rejoice in it less for me than for your poor mother. I'll rejuvenate he, and she won't rant any longer, for beauty renders a woman good-humored, and I remember that my poor wife didn't rant at eighteen, when I married her, as she rants at forty-five, as she has since last April."

The beautiful Hhûhhuip maintained a respectful silence, not wishing either to lie out of complaisance or to argue any longer with her dear father.

And the father and daughter went into the apartment of His Crunching Highness the Great Hihouhâh, Duc of the Yellow Wolves, which was also in jet and sumptuously furnished. There was a fine breakfast, which was copiously furnished with topaz liquor by ewes as white as snow.

"Well, my Father," said the Great Yellow Wolf, "You see now what the fate of your second daughter is. She has recovered her original beauty and has everything she wishes; do you think she has anything to mourn?

"Oh, she's even more fortunate than my eldest," Brancabanda replied, "And I'm burning with desire to return to my poor wife to tell her all this and rejuvenate her with your jelly.

"Have the chariot prepared!" Hihouhâh shouted to his white sheep, "for I can't keep my Father any longer without causing pain to my Mother. Look, here's a pot of jelly; one spoonful should suffice at first for our Mother; your provisions will be packed up, with two large flasks of topaz liquor."

"Much obliged, my Son-in-law."

"You see," added His Crunching Highness the Great Wolf, "how full of prudence my conduct is; I protect the white sheep, my subjects; everything that breathes in my Estates has a father in me, and like all other Kings, I eat my neighbors."

"Oh, the fine lad, the fine lad!" said Brancabanda. "What a pity he's a wolf!"

"Oh, Father, you find evil in us what you approve in humans, who do a hundred time more of it every day than wolves—but let's leave it there. You can see that with the flesh of my captures I make excellent stews; with the bones, the jelly that rejuvenates; the teeth, prepared in my fashion, become turquoises; my ewes furnish me with ambrosia and their faeces, compressed into tablets, becomes the ebony of which the palace is built.

My ram doorkeeper furnishes me with jet. I trade with my brothers-in-law; we exchange the things that we lack mutually; that's why I have such beautiful Coqueliquette mirrors."

The visitor was even more amazed than in the home of his eldest daughter the beautiful Hhûeip. He embraced his son-on-law the yellow wolf twice, and his daughter a hundred times; and, blessing Heaven for having given his eldest daughter as a wife to a dog, and his second daughter in marriage to a wolf, he climbed into the chariot that had brought him, for the white lamb had been whistled to summon him back from his occupations, and he was already on the seat.

"Adieu, my Father!"

"Adieu, my daughter! Adieu, my Son-in-law!"

"Au revoir," added the Great Wolf, affectionately, "And don't lose the ivory talisman, for there's only your son-in-law the dog who can give you one."

The chariot had already departed; the white sheep were going like the wind, and at ten o'clock in the evening, they deposited Brancabanda at his door, with all the fine presents he had brought.

"Houssihoussa, my poor wife, open the door for your husband," he shouted.

"Is that you, Brancabanda?"

"Yes, it's me, who has come back from seeing our son-in-law, His Crunching Highness the Yellow Wolf and our daughter Her Serene Highness Hhûhhuip, Duchesse of Wolves, Lady of the beautiful city of Wolfville, etc., etc., who is more beautiful than ever."

The good woman heard that, and came to open the door, joyfully.

But when she saw, instead of her husband, a handsome young Monsieur of twenty years, very elegant, with a fine braided coat and the rest, the candle fell from her hands.

"You're not my husband," she said to him, "but apparently some good genius."

"It's me," replied Brancabanda. "My son-in-law His Crunching Highness the Yellow Wolf had given me a jelly of bones of Flemish sheep, Prussian deer and English boar, which rejuvenates and makes the teeth grow back."

The good woman heard that, picked up the candle, relit it, and then came to threw her arms around her husband, saying to him: "Give me the rejuvenating jelly quickly; I'll see the rest later..."

Brancabanda had a little jar of it in his pocket; he gave a spoonful to Houssihoussa. She asked for more.

I'm not risking anything, he said to himself. *A woman can't be too young.* And he gave her four spoonfuls in succession, instead of one. What was his astonishment! One spoonful had brought her back from forty-five to thirty-five, the second to twenty-five, the third to fifteen; the fourth put her back on the apron-strings.

"Oh, my God!" said Brancabanda. "What have I done? I wanted to have a young wife and she's no more than an infant."

Poor Houssihoussa immediately stated making dolls, coiffing them, feeding them pap and whipping them when she supposed them to be naughty. Her husband, much afflicted, put away all the provisions he had brought, gave his wife supper, laid her down in a cradle that had once served for their children, rocked her, and put her to bed when she fell asleep. That was what came of not being able to moderate a wife who wanted to become young again!

The following day, Brancabanda was greatly embarrassed. He wanted to go and see his other two daughters, but how could he leave little Houssihoussa alone? He thought about that all day, and his anxieties increased instead of diminishing. The child was always on the move; she played with the fire, she threw everything out of the bedroom, or she went to make ripples in the well with her saliva, at the risk of falling in, etc., etc., etc.

In the end, after a week, by dint of meditation, he thought of making a large parrot-cage with provisions for two days, of locking all the doors and departing immediately to go to see his dear Bizibizibizi, his third daughter, the wife of His Crested Eminence the Greatest of Cocks.

Thus, having arranged everything, he took his ivory talisman and tapped it on the threshold of the door, saying: "By the crest of my son-in-law His Crested Eminence the Great Blue Cock, may his chariot be here, harnessed as he intends."

Brancabanda had no sooner pronounced those words than he perceived something like a large white cloud in the air, which gradually descended, no longer appearing as anything but a large cage of silver wire attached at the four corners to four ropes of blue and silver silk, to each of which were harnessed six storks, six cranes and six wild geese. At the front was a little seat made of a single ruby, on which the white blackbird was perched, holding in its break a golden thread at delicate as a hair, with which it was directing the flight of the large birds that were carrying the cage. Brancabanda could see that the vehicle was for him; he told little

Houssihoussa to be good, gave her some toys, showed her the provisions, kissed her and left.

"You've changed a great deal, Seigneur Brancabanda," the white blackbird sad to him.

"Alas yes, I've been rejuvenated; but having also wanted to rejuvenate my wife, the god Houssihoussa, I've returned her to infancy."

"Rejuvenated?" The white blackbird said, laughing as one whistles comically. "Rejuvenated like that...but didn't you do what His Crunching Highness Hihouhâh prescribed?"

"Yes, yes, handsome white blackbird, and more."

"More, Seigneur Brancabanda! There's the snag! *It's necessary not to do too much.* But the harm can't be beyond remedy."

Thus spoke the white blackbird, but then he quit his passenger in order to go and direct the wild geese, which were straying off course.

Then Brancabanda, thus elevated, started considering from high in the air the fields, the forests the rivers and sea that fled beneath his feet He saw lands where girls were sold secretly in bedrooms, others where they were sold in public in the market; others where there were black people, others where there were yellow ones, others where there were copper-colored ones; others where humans were hunted, and then given to the dogs; others where there were monkeys instead of humans; others where there were only dogs. That was the land in which his son-in-law His Mordant Highness the green dog was a Marquis, for he saw the ivory palace, and even the beautiful Hhûeip, his daughter, who was walking in the park followed by her chambermaids the doe-rabbits—which gave him a great deal of pleasure, but he passed over too quickly to be able to talk to her.

Afterwards he saw the land of the wolves, of which his son-in-law His Crunching Highness Hihouhâh was Duc, and the palace of ebony, and the Great Wolf himself, lying in ambush at a corner of a wood; he saw him fall, with his hunting foxes, on a flock of Flemish sheep, which they ravaged. Transported with joy on seeing his son-on-law kill two big German sheepdogs and an English sheepdog that had attacked him, Brancabanda clapped his hands and was about to cry: "Courage!" but the white blackbird put a foot over his mouth to impose silence, saying to him:

"It's necessary that the world doesn't know very much about the powers of the fays; it would render other humans jealous, and every day, instead of laboring, they'd amuse themselves making futile wishes. That's why the fays hide their favors; for, as they appear to be matters of chance, no one can procure them, and they arrive the least to those who desire them the most."

Brancabanda was glad to know that, and resume looking, without saying anything. Finally, he perceived a land where the cities were in the trees and the houses were constructed in the form of chicken-coops. In the middle of the city he distinguished a superb palace made in the form of a domed cage; it was seated on four enormous chestnut-trees, each of which was as large as those of Etna.[20]

The palace was a thousand feet in circumference and was entirely made of gold wire; the dome, with little azure columns of the Corinthian order, with sapphire capitals, composed a superb apartment, but into which the eye could not penetrate, for it was entirely garnished

---

[20] Author's note: "One of the chestnut-trees of Etna is two hundred and four feet in circumference."

with mirrors and fine curtains of green taffeta with gold fringes.

The flying cage stopped above the great city of Coqueliquette, the capital of His Crested Eminence the Great Cocodinq, Prince of Cocks, opposite the main door of the dome of the palace. The white blackbird whistled. Immediately, a superb peacock ornamented by a rich baldric—for he was Swiss by nation—decorated with precious stones came to see what it was.

"Tell our mistress the Supremely Eminent Princess, the beautiful Bizibizibizi. That I've brought the very elevated Seigneur Brancabanda, who is here."

As soon as the beautiful Bizibizibizi heard someone tell the doorman about the arrival of her father, she ran to meet him in spite of etiquette, accompanied by twenty-four pheasants, her chambermaids.

"Oh, it's my dear Father," she said to him, holding out her hand to help him out of his aerial carriage and then throwing herself into his arms..

The visitor only recognized her by her voice as the beautiful Bizibizibizi, his third daughter; so light and delicate was she, although she had already been very much so before. She had also become so beautiful, and she was so covered in rubies and admirably clustered stones that she dazzled him. Even the pheasants had tiaras and necklaces.

"Bonsoir, my dear daughter," said Brancabanda, so very emotional that he was weeping with pleasure. "You seem very delicate, my dear child."

"I'm only lighter, Papa. And my dear Maman?"

"Alas, she's excessively rejuvenated, for she's an infant, for having eaten too much jelly of bones of Flemish sheep, Prussian deer and English boar. And you, my daughter, are you as happy as your sister Hhûeip, who married his Mordant Highness the Marquis Ouapouahoup, the nimblest of the green dogs, although, in truth, he's fatter than a bulldog, and your sister Hhûhhuip, who married His Crunching Highness Monseigneur le Duc Hihouhâh, the best sovereign the yellow wolves have ever had, although he's something of a thief?

"I have everything I wish, dear Father."

"And your husband, where is he?"

"He's out on the dung-heaps, looking for worms for our supper."

"What's that, my Daughter! Poor dear, poor dear! I can easily see that you're the unfortunate one!"

The beautiful Bizibizibizi started smiling with so much grace and tenderness that all nature smiled with her.

"You'll taste it, Father."

"God preserve me from that!" So saying, he darted a glance at the lovely pheasants, but dared not say: "There's something that would make me a nice supper."

"If that doesn't suit you, Father, I'll order my swallows to catch you some flies, which are better than ortolans; and tell my sparrows to trap cockchafers and crickets, which taste a hundred times more exquisite than Le Mans capons and Gâtinois turkeys."

None of that tempted Brancabanda. He shook his head; but, remembering that he was in his son-in-law's house, he was prepared to be patient.

"My God, Papa," his daughter said to him, "how changed you are!"

"That's because I've been rejuvenated."

"Rejuvenated! On the contrary!"

"How am I not rejuvenated?"

"You look about twenty-five, but you're as fat as a man of forty."

"My child, it's necessary to tell you about the adventure that your mother and I have had. My son-in-law the yellow wolf, your brother-in-law, gave me, as I told you, the jelly of bones of Flemish sheep, Prussian deer and English boar, which rejuvenates and makes teeth grow back."

"Teeth? Why make teeth?"

"But my child, to chew, and I'm very glad to have them."

"Here, Father, look. Do I have a single one?"

Brancabanda was quite astonished. He looked into the mouth of the beautiful Bizibizibizi, his third daughter, and instead of teeth, he saw two beautiful rows of Oriental pearls.

"That's much better...," he started to say, "but to finish our story, my son-in-law the yellow wolf rejuvenated me, albeit a trifle stoutly, since you insist, with a half-spoonful of jelly, and as women are apparently a little more difficult to rejuvenate, he told me to give a whole one to your poor mother; but she asked me for more; wanting to do good and not to be mean, I gave her four, without waiting for the first to have its full effect. Now, instead of a wife, I no longer have anything but an infant of three or four, who plays with dolls, messes about with the fire at the risk of burning herself and makes ripples in the well with her saliva at the risk of falling in."

"Oh, my dear little Maman" said Bizibizibizi, quivering with joy, "how I'd like to have her here, to bounce her on my knees. Will she grow old? It's necessary to keep giving her the jelly, so that she always stays as she is...but my husband's very late. I'll go and call him."

She advanced to the door of her apartment, where she started to call: "*Quitt, quitt, pithoûh, pithoûh*" My father has come! My father has come!"

She had no sooner said that than a great cock-a-doodle-doo was heard, so loud that it made all the gold and silver wire composing the great palace cage vibrate, and all those of the cage-houses of the city of Coqueliquette, like the strings of a spinet,[21] which produced a delightful harmony.

"He's coming, my dear Papa. In the meantime, tell me, if you please, what you did when my sisters and I had gone, and His Majesty King Bêhêhê had carried off Hhouiphhouip, my youngest sister—for we saw them going past here, but weren't able to talk to her."

"We were very chagrined, my child," Brancabanda replied to his daughter, "and I thought of you every day, saying: 'Alas, alas! So I had four daughters, as beautiful as the day, as dexterous as fays, for a dog to tear apart the eldest, a wolf to crunch the second, a cock to peck the third and a red sheep to brose the youngest!"

Then he told his daughter everything that had happened to him until the present moment. He had just finished when the peacock doorman whistled—and immediately, Bizibizibizi got up in order to run to meet her husband.

"My dear Cocodinq," she said to him, in a soft and harmonious voice. "Here's my Father, who has come to see us. Have you scratched well? Oh, what beautiful worms! They're more than an ell long!"

---

[21] There is an untranslatable pun here; the French *épinette* [spinet] also means "hen-coop."

"Cocococococodinq!—that is the "parbleu" of cocks of all colors—"Bonsoir, my Father! Let me embrace you!"

And they embraced, wing over arm.

"Bonsoir, my son-in-law."

"Are you well, my Father?"

"Marvelous, since I began to see my daughters again, and especially since my son-in-law the yellow wolf, your brother-in-law, gave me a jelly that has rejuvenated me."

"And our worthy Mother?"

"Alas, she's excessively rejuvenated."

"There's no great harm in that, my Father; I'll give you the milk of a confined hen,[22] every spoonful of which ages by five years."

"Oh, you'd give me great pleasure, my son-in-law."

During this conversation, the vulture cocks accommodated the worms, and as the kitchens were underneath the cage, the sweet odor of delicate dishes rose all the way up to Bizibizibizi's apartment.

"What's that I can smell?" asked Brancabanda. "That's an odor that awakens my appetite. It's better than what your husband just brought, isn't it?"

"I'm delighted that the odor pleases you, my Father," said His Crested Eminence Cocodinq, Prince of

---

[22] The French *lait de poule*, which translates literally as "hen's milk," refers to an "egg flip" or some other drinkable mixture of eggs and milk, often sugared. However, its particular use in this story involves a play on words that will subsequently be explained by Cocodinq, which will also explain the seemingly-eccentric inclusion here of the word *recluse* [confined], so I have employed a literal translation. Restif had no idea, of course, that "battery hens" would one day be kept in close confinement on a routine basis.

164

the Blue Cocks, laughing. At the same time, an eagle, carver-waiter to Her Serene Eminence Bizibizibizi, Princess of Coqueliquette, capital of the land of the blue cocks, came with a napkin around its neck to announce to the sovereign that dinner was served.

They went into the dining room, where the first course was a blue eel, but so well prepared that the visitor agreed that he has never eaten anything as good, even in the homes of his son-in-law the Green Dog and his son-in-law the Great Yellow Wolf. Afterwards, excellent sea- and fresh-water fish were served, in accordance with what Brancabanda asked for, although they were still the same foodstuffs.

"A drink!" crowed His Crested Eminence Prince Cocodinq—for in the land of the cocks one says "crowed" rather than "said"—and two herons brought pure water in beautiful chrysolite cups. Princess Bizibizibizi dropped half a spoonful of confined-hen's-milk into her father's cup and invited him to drink.

Where is the carcass-water of my son-in-law Oupahoup, the visitor wondered, silently, *or the water topazed by white ewes of my son-in-law Hihouhâh?* And if he had not been strangled by thirst, I believe that he would not have drunk, for the fellow, although he was a young French fop, did not like water. But as soon as he had tasted the delicious liquor mixed with confined-hen's-milk he changed his mind. He drank so much of it, in spite of the representations of his daughter and his son-in-law Cocodinq, always putting more confined-hen's-milk into it, that his belly became as fat as a beer-barrel.

Finally, Bizibizibizi asked for the dessert. His Created Eminence Cocodinq got up and told a duck, his dish-washer, to prepare a large space in the silver hearth of the room where they were eating. And when the hearth was clean, Cocoding set himself above it, bent his legs, made a fan of his beautiful tail, stretched out his handsome colored neck and did the opposite of eating, which filled the hearth with a golden yellow substance, which the duck covered with a gilded silver pie-dish lid.

Brancabanda was very surprised by what his son-in-law, His Crested Eminence Cocodinq, had just done, who said to him: "Well, my Father, how did you find our feast?"

"Excellent."

"That's nothing; the pie that is cooking, whose perfume you can already smell, is a dish far above anything my two brothers-in-law you can have given you to eat."

"I believe so, but I won't have any of it..."

The blue cock and the Princess, his wife, started to laugh, and the duck went to uncover the pie in order to serve it on a beautiful gold platter, but less beautiful than the pie, which had no sooner been exposed to the air than an appetizing aroma, better than anything a human gourmand's nose had ever smelled, came to embalm Brancabanda's. He was overjoyed.

"Can you smell that, Papa?" the beautiful Bizibizibizi said to him.

"Let's see, then," the visitor replied, reopening his knife, which he had already closed. And as soon as he had tasted the pie he never ceased to declare how good it was—to such an extent that if he had not already eaten too much he would not have left a crumb, even if it weighed a good forty pounds.

He drank a few more cups of water mingled with confined-hen's-milk, and when he had supped well—vey well—the beautiful Bizibizibizi, followed by the white blackbird, took her Papa, who could no longer

166

stand upright, to sleep in a beautiful cage of golden wire lined with white satin, garnished with beautiful Coqueliquette mirrors, which are the most beautiful in the entire world, in golden frames enriched with rubies.

Brancabanda, who could not move his hands or feet, was undressed by the young pheasants, who laid him down on in a beautiful bed of white damask with golden trimmings, with their mistress's monogram in rubies. The mattress was the finest down of humming-birds, and the white blackbird perched on one of the golden curtain-rails of the bed. The fellow slept profoundly and only woke up in broad daylight, to the song of the white blackbird, nightingales, canaries, finches and warblers, who gave him a very pretty concert.

As soon as Brancabanda was fully awake he searched for his clothes, but instead of his beautiful braided coat in the French style he found a complete Persian outfit lavishly sown with rubies and pearls.

"That's for you," said the white blackbird, "for the attire ought to be proportional to the figure and character. Adieu, I'm going to where my duty calls me, but I'll return when you need me." And he flew out of the window.

Brancabanda got dressed promptly, and, thinking about how he had left little Houssihoussa in a parrot-cage, resolved to leave as soon as he had had breakfast.

As soon as movement was heard in his room, Her Serene Eminence the delicate Bizibizibizi's pheasants came to receive his orders, but on seeing him dressed they withdrew.

Brancabanda, while waiting for the beautiful Bizibizibizi, wife of His Crested Eminence Cocodinq, the Greatest of Cocks, to get up, was curious to see all the beauties of the palace cage, proposing to himself no longer to have any deference for Spanish grandees like those in the house of his son-in-law the dog, or to get angry with French fops who spat in the face of an old man, like those in the house of his son-in-law the wolf. But it is necessary not to swear to anything.

On going to open his door, which slid in grooves, as in other cages, he had no sooner lifted the curtain of white satin that masked it than he perceived in the cage opposite his own a grave old man who was also about to slide his door, and who appeared be about two hundred years old.

Struck by that venerable aspect, Brancabanda thought that it was appropriate for a young man like him, who had a wife who played with dolls and made ripples with her saliva in a well, to be polite. He bowed profoundly. The old man did the same, so profoundly that his long beard, whiter than wild chicory, touched the floor. Then Brancabanda stepped forward to go out. The old man, doubtless shocked by that lack of consideration on the part of a young man, advanced at the same time, with the result that Brancabanda and he collided head-on like two rams.

Brancabanda sensed that he was in the wrong and stepped back politely. The old man did the same. Brancabanda bowed and invited him to go first. The old man, doubtless sorry for is initial vivacity, did as much—with the consequence that Brancabanda, who was in a hurry, wanting to return quickly after breakfast to little Houssihoussa, whom he had left in a cage, advanced precipitately in order to put an end to the pantomime. But the old man, who had apparently not expected that he would yield so swiftly, did the same, and they collided with so much violence that they both fell backwards.

Transported by anger, and feeling a huge bump on his forehead, Brancabanda picked up a platinum pike with a golden shaft that was nearby and launched himself at the reckless old Persian, who had not been knocked unconscious. At the double thrust of the two champions, the mirror—for it was one of those that formed the sliding door—shattered, and Brancabanda had the glory of putting his adversary to flight, for he was no longer apparent.

In the meantime, the pheasants, the Princess's chambermaids, had gone to inform the beautiful Bizibizibizi that Seigneur Brancabanda, her very elevated father, was ready; and that respectful daughter had dressed in haste in order to come and salute the author of her days. She arrived just at the time that he poor fellow, proud of his victory over the old Persian, was sitting on the debris of the mirror, as if on trophies.

"What's the matter, my dear Papa?" she said to him. "You're quite distressed."

Brancabanda told her how he had seen an old man who occupied the cage next door, who was surely a magician; how he had saluted him; how he had saluted him; how he had tried to get past; how they had collided; how they had got angry; how they had fought; and how he had won a complete victory over his enemy, magician as he was, since he had forced him to disappear, without the slightest trace of him being visible. He added, modestly, that there was, however, no great glory for a young man like him to have vanquished an old man who appeared to be at least two hundred years old.

The beautiful Bizibizibizi did not understand any of what the very elevated Seigneur her father said. Fortunately, His Crested Eminence the Great Cocodinq arrived, who said to the visitor:

169

"That old man was yourself, Father, of whom the mirror of your door reflected the image."

"Bah!" said Brancabanda, laughing. "Get away! You're trying to make me believe that balloons are lanterns. I saw, separate from me, an old man—and am I not young?

"Father," said Cocodinq, "I respect you too much to impose upon you. I told you yesterday that the confined-hen's-milk led to maturity, just as the jelly of my brother-in-law His Crunching Yellow Highness Hihouhâh returns to childhood. In spite of that, at supper, you drank it endlessly, and this is the result; if we'd let you have your own way, you'd be two thousand years old rather than two hundred."

At the same time, Cocodinq, Prince of Cocks, picked up a shard of the broken mirror, in which the poor fellow saw himself, as well as the others, and he would have been frightened by his antiquity if he had really been certain that it was him, but he was still in some doubt.

"Observe, dear Father," continued His Crested Eminence the Great Cocodinq, "that neither I nor the Princess of Cocks, my wife, put hen's milk in our cups; pure water is the beverage of nature; it is made for our bodies. If one watered a plant with liqueurs, they would dry it up; of that, as of all pleasures, one should only take a little: *nothing to excess* is a maxim I habitually follow, and, Cock as I am, my wife can give you news of it. But there's a remedy for everything; let's go and have breakfast."

"Yes," said Brancabanda, sadly, "for it's necessary for me to return very quickly to my dear Houssihoussa, whom I left in a cage, and who will take care of my old age. A curse on mirrors, and their inventor!"

They went into the apartment-cage of His Crested Eminence the Great Blue Cock, where a pie was served like that of the previous evening, and the remains of both, as well as many other provisions, were packed up in order to be taken away by the visitor to little Houssihoussa. Brancabanda drank, but he no longer wanted confined-hen's milk; nevertheless, he found the beverage very agreeable.

"You see how we live, Father," said Cocodinq; "everything becomes for us a delicate food; with a little preparation, the tails of our peacocks change into rubies, from the eggs of our pigeons I occasionally make pearls, and it's me who has furnished those that my brothers-in-law, the Great Dog and the Great Wolf, have. In exchange, they give me ivory, ebony and all their productions. His Two-Horned Majesty pays me in gold, etc. I also furnish them with those beautiful Coqueliquette mirrors, known throughout green dog, yellow wolf, blue cock and red sheep society. I'll tell you now how I make them.

"The hen's-milk that you drank is taken from the eggs of all the hens condemned to celibacy, who live here in nunneries; as it is forbidden from them to reproduce, we break all their eggs and throw them into a great vat; we let them ferment and then we take out the clear liquid that floats on the top, called hen's-milk. With the white I make those beautiful mirrors, and as for the yolk, it changes into a kind of bread, with which we nourish all the capons, my former rivals, whom I've had confined in monasteries, where they enrage my wellbeing. As for all my other subjects of the volatile folk, I govern them with wisdom and bounty, from the eagle that soars above the clouds to the mosquito that buzzes around the candle, and they all cherish me.

"Oh, the fine fellow! What a fine fellow of a Prince my son-in-law His Crested Eminence is!" exclaimed Brancabanda. "What a pity that such an honest fellow is a cock..."

His Crested Eminence Cocodinq burst out laughing, saying: "When vigilance and marital dignity quit humans they took refuge among us, my Father. Anyway, how does our lot seem to you at present?"

"I find it even more fortunate than that of my eldest daughter, the wife of His Mordant Highness the Great Green Dog, and that of my second daughter, the spouse of His Crunching Highness the Great Yellow Wolf. I even presume that it must surpass that of my youngest, the spouse of His Two-Horned Majesty the Great Red Sheep. I see, with consolation that you live in good intelligence and that you make a good household with your wives. How, though, have you rendered them so beautiful?"

"By contentment, my Father, for that's what embellishes a spouse most of all."

"That's not a bad thing to know...but it's a little late," he added, touching his beard, "and I'd prefer not to have become so old; and also that you—all four of my sons-in-law—might become a little more human?"

"That doesn't depend on us," said the Great Blue Cock, sighing. "As regards your old age, Father, when you get home, it's necessary to give our good Mother a few half spoonfuls of hen's milk, until she reaches the age at which you want her to remain, and at the same time, you take double doses of the jelly my brother-in-law His Crunching Highness the Yellow Wolf gave you, alternating with your wife, until you return to your natural age—no less; remember that well, for otherwise, something bad might happen—and then throw the rest of the jelly in the fire. Lock the hen's milk away in a chest, though, and give the key to your wife. Adieu, my dear Father, and look after the talisman, in order to come to see us again, for only brother-in-law Oupouahoup can provide one."

"Adieu, my children, and much obliged," said Brancabanda, "for I'm ready to depart."

And the golden cage borne by the storks, the cranes and the geese having been loaded with provisions, they whistled for the white blackbird, who came back immediately from far away and took the reins. Brancabanda climbed into it, and was immediately lifted above the clouds.

In the evening, he arrived at his house; the storks unloaded the presents, and the empty cage returned.

Brancabanda opened the door and found little Houssihoussa with her body half-passed through the brass wires of the cage, almost suffocated. He hastened to detach her and bring her round. Scarcely had she recovered her senses, however, than she uttered a cry of fright, occasioned by the old age and costume of her husband, whom he did not recognize. He tried to make her take the hen's milk, in order to render her more reasonable, but the child rejected it with all her force, as if mechanically. Half the night passed without him being able to make her take a single drop.

Finally, by dint of screaming, the child went to sleep, overcome by exhaustion and lassitude.

I could swear, Brancabanda thought, *that she knows, by an instinct natural to women, that it makes one older, but we'll see, now that she's asleep...* And he separated her teeth with a knife, and then put half a spoonful of hen's milk into her mouth, while he took a spoonful of his wolf son-in-law's jelly.

The child appeared to be fifteen. "How pretty she is!" he said, kissing her. "What if I leave her there...?" He was strongly tempted to do that, but, having looked in one of the fragments of the mirror that he had broken in the home of his crested son-in-law, the Great Cocodinq while fighting against the Persian magician, which he had brought back out of curiosity, he found that he was still a hundred and fifty years old.

What can I do? he thought. *She wouldn't be able to suffer me.* He gave her another half-spoonful and took a spoonful of jelly himself; his wife appeared to be thirty.

That's a formed beauty, he thought, then. *Let's leave her like that...* Then he looked at his own face, to see whether it was passable. He was no longer more than a hundred. *I'm still too old.*

He gave a third half-spoonful to his wife, and the good Houssihoussa was forty-five years old. *What use has the jelly been to me? Now my wife's as she was before...* Then he took the spoonful, and found himself fifty-five years old, as on the day when he had set off to visit his son-in-law, His Crunching Highness the Yellow Wolf.

Brancabanda immediately threw in the fire all the jelly of the Flemish sheep, Prussian deer and English boar bones, as his crested son-in-law Cocodinq had instructed, and he locked the rest of the hen's milk in a chest, the key to which he put in his wife's pocket—for her clothing had diminished and regrown exactly like her. Then he woke her up.

"Oh, my dear man, where have you come from?"

"From the home of my son-in-law the Blue Cock."

"My God! I had a funny dream during your voyage! I dreamed that I was no more than three years old, and I was still making dolls."

"That wasn't a dream, though!" And he started to tell her everything: how he had returned her to infancy with the jelly of his son-in-law the Great Hihouhâh the Yellow Wolf; how he had grown old in the house of his crested son-in-law the Great Cocodinq, Prince of the Blue Cocks by drinking too much confined-hens; milk; how he had wanted to bring her back to the age of reason and resume it with her; and how he had returned both of them to the way they were before."

Houssihoussa had a great deal of difficulty letting him finish; she started weeping, wailing and tearing out her hair, saying: "What a villainous old swine! Because he was told he had to make me old too! No, I'll never console myself, and I'd rather die than remain old all my life, as I am. Oh, if I hadn't fallen asleep, you'd have seen—you'd have seen how I'd have taken your satanic confined-hens' milk! Behold the villainous traitor, who played that trick on me while I was asleep!"

Her husband said everything that he could say to make her listen to reason, but he never succeeded. In end, however, as they were both hungry, they had supper, and Cocodinq's excellent pie calmed the doors and regret of the good Houssihoussa, for the moment.

When they had eaten well, the wife said to her husband; "Have you still got any of that accursed hen's milk?"

"Yes, but I've locked it in your chest and put the key in your pocket."

"So much the better, so much the better!" she said, laughing. "It'll last a long time. And the jelly," she added, simpering a little. "Is there much left?"

"I threw it in the fire."

"Oh, you accursed hell-toad!" cried Houssihoussa—and she started lamenting again. When she had lamented again for a long time, she went to sleep until it was broad daylight the next day, unable to console herself for having passed in a single night from the age of three, when she had amused herself making dolls, to that of forty-five, when she was no longer able to amuse herself with anything.

One wearies of everything, Brancabanda thought, *and my wife will doubtless weary of crying...*

But he was greatly mistaken. A woman who regrets her youth is never consoled. She cried the next day, the day after, the fourth day, the fifth, and would probably be crying still if Brancabanda had not thought of an expedient.

The provisions that he had brought were beginning to run out.

"Now, my dear wife," he said, "call a truce in your complaints in order to listen to me; you can start again afterwards if you want to."

"Oh, you wretch!" his wife said. "You've made me old and you want me to shut up! No, no, no, no, no, no, no—a hundred times no, a thousand, ten thousand, a million times no! I won't shut up!"

Fortunately, the fit of rage into which she had flown caused her to lose her voice, with the consequence that he was free to speak.

"This is what I wanted to say to you," he went on. "My son-in-law the Great Yellow Wolf gave me a rejuvenating jelly, my crested son-in-law Cocodinq the hen's milk that ages; perhaps my son-in-law the Red Sheep has something that re-rejuvenates when one has already been rejuvenated before. Now that our provisions are

176

running out, I'm going to take my ivory talisman and rap on the threshold of our door."

"Oh," said Houssihoussa in an extinct voice, "I'll never be three years old again. But in sum, what you say consoles me a little and I'll await your return impatiently. And then, if it doesn't succeed, won't we still have our son-in-law the yellow wolf?"

Brancabanda, seeing Houssihoussa slightly consoled, took his ivory talisman and raped on the threshold of the door, saying: "By the double horn of my son-in-law Bêhêhê, His Two-Horned Majesty the King of the Red Sheep, may his chariot be here, harnessed as he intends."

No sooner had the fellow pronounced those words than he perceived a great cloud of dust in the far distance, on the road. It drew nearer and nearer, until, in the end, he saw a beautiful golden chariot that appeared to be moving of its own accord, except that visible on the seat was the yellow-red-blue-green muskrat, whose paw was holding reins of green-and-gold silk no thicker than a thread. Finally, when the chariot was very close, Brancabanda perceived that it was being drawn by twelve thousand rats, buried in a dust-cloud.

He saw that it was the vehicle he had requested. He embraced Houssihoussa and leapt lightly into the golden chariot.

The rats turned round and started running more rapidly than the wind, until they reached the sea. When they reached the sea the yellow-red-blue-green muskrat got down from his seat and rubbed the muzzles of all the rats with his musk-pouch—which was done in the blink of an eye, so quickly did he move; and as he rubbed they were conglomerated, and when they had all been rubbed and conglomerated, there was a huge whale; the twelve thousand reins were twisted into a stout cable, which the ash-blonde-red-blue-green muskrat held in his paw as easily as before. The huge whale loaded the chariot on to its back and traversed the ocean like an arrow.

As soon as the ocean had been crossed, the yellow-red-blue-green muskrat rubbed the muzzle of the huge whale with its musk-pouch and all the rats were immediately deconglomerated, the stout cable wound up into little threads of green and gold silk, and the chariot rolled on again instead of floating.

"Handsome yellow-red-blue-green muskrat," said Brancabanda to his coachman, "Metamorphoses cost you nothing, and the one you've just made raises my hopes. My poor wife is in despair at no longer being a three-year-old girl who plays with dolls and makes ripples in the well with her saliva; if you can change twelve thousand rats into a whale and a whale into twelve thousand rats, it ought to be even easier for you to change an old woman into a little girl?"

"No, no, excellent Seigneur," the yellow-red-blue-green muskrat replied. "The King, His doubly-horned Bêhêhêêê, the most beautiful of the Red Sheep, my noble master, husband of Her Gracious Majesty Queen Hhouiphhouip, the youngest of Your Excellency's daughters, has great power, and we obtain all of ours from him; but it is not permitted for us to penetrate into the august sanctuary of his sublime two-horned thoughts, nor to say what His High and Royal Majesty might do or not do..."

Brancabanda was stunned by that fine speech, and said to himself: *How much intelligence there must be in the kingdom of the Red Sheep, if a simple muskrat, a coachman by trade, speaks in such a pompous and beau-*

tiful manner! And the fellow, who was flabbergasted, resolved to keep silent for the rest of the journey.

On the stroke of midnight, counting the hours as a clock located in Charmelieu would have marked them, but at four o'clock in the afternoon local time, given that it was in the occident and the whale-rat had traveled as rapidly as the Sun, Brancabanda discovered a great city in the middle of a vast prairie, which appeared from a distance to be on fire.

He could not retain himself. "Sage and discreet yellow-red-blue-green muskrat, what do I see there? It seems to me that it's a city burning?"

The muskrat started guioring, saying: "In a country governed by the unerring wisdom of His all-seeing Two-Horned Majesty Bêhêhêêêê, there is no disorder, and the conflagration of a city would be one. In a moment, Your Excellency will know what it is."

"But can't you tell me?"

"Seigneur, if all the sovereigns in the world had rats as discreet and laconic as me for counselors, their secrets would never be laid bare..."

As he finished speaking, they arrived, and Brancabanda perceived that what he had mistaken for a city on fire was a city built entirely of agate, covered in gold, in the middle of which was a crystal palace roofed with rubies. He therefore went into the beautiful city of Mêhêhê, which was paved with silver, and the chariot stopped in front of the superb crystal palace, paved with gold, whose columns of the Composite Order had emerald capitals perfectly imitating the foliage of oak-trees; the shafts were amethyst and the grooves were of delicately-shaded gems, and as the whole edifice was covered in rubies, it had the appearance of an ardent brazier in the middle of the city.

A huge green monkey with a rich baldric—for he was Swiss by nation—sown with all possible gemstones, came in response to the muskrat Iouriri Yellow-red-green-blue's call and made two topaz doors garnished with chrysoprase studs rotate on platinum hinges. Then he whistled.

A green she-monkey, magnificently dressed, whose tail was carried by twenty-four blue mice with diamond collars, presented herself on a golden balcony. "Who is it?" she said.

"His Excellency the very noble, very elevated, very great, very powerful, very wise, very just, very strong and very old Seigneur, Monseigneur de Brancabanda, the King's son-in-law and father of Her Imperial Majesty, the very young, very beautiful, very gracious, very light, very intelligent, very coquettish and very clement Lady the Queen Hhouiphhouip, the dust of whose feet I kiss very humbly, Sovereign of the noble city built of Agate and covered in gold, Mistress of the crystal palace whose roof is made of rubies, etc., etc., etc., etc., etc., etc., a million time etc."

After that proclamation, the beautiful green she-monkey and the twenty blue mice made a profound curtsy, and went back inside to inform the Queen.

As soon as the beautiful Hhouiphhouip had been informed of her father's arrival she got up, transported by joy, and without observing etiquette or waiting for the green she-monkeys, her maids of honor, to pick up her train, she ran precipitately to meet her father.

"Ah" It's my dear Papa!" he cried, extending her hand to help him down from the golden chariot. Then she threw herself into his arms.

Utterly dazzled the visitor only recognized the beautiful Hhouiphhouip, his youngest daughter, by her voice, so beautiful had she become again, loupinette as she had been, and so brilliant was the glare of the diamonds that covered her from head to toe. Even her green she-monkeys were laden with them and one might have taken their mistress for a Sun surrounded by stars.

"My dear Father, how glad I am to see you again! And Maman?"

"She'd be quite well at present, if she weren't annoyed by having grown old again." As he said that, he could not weary of looking at the beautiful Hhouiphhouip and admiring her. "Oh, my dear daughter, you appear to me to be richer than all your sisters, but are you more fortunate?

"I've seen your sister the Marquise Hhûeip, who married the worthy Seigneur His Mordant Highness Marquis Ouapouahoup, the nimblest of the green dogs, although, in truth he's fatter than a bulldog, who is happy, although her husband nourishes her on carcasses.

"I've seen your sister Duchess Hhûhhuip, who married His Crunching Highness Monseigneur Duc Hihouhâh, the noblest of the yellow wolves, for he descends from King Limaçon and one of his grandmothers was nurse to a pope named Mameus—I say pope because he was King of Rome, and everyone knows that that's the pope—who is very happy, although her husband only nourishes her on raw meat and only gives her the piss of white ewes to drunk.

"I've seen your sister Princess Bizibizibizi, the wife of Monseigneur His Crested Eminence the Prince of the Blue Cocks, who reins in Conquelliquete, where the most beautiful magics possible are made, from which Spanish grandees emerge, as well as French fops who spit in everyone's face and then draw their swords, and Persian old men who, after being polite, fight with pike-thrusts, although I made the latter see reason, who is very happy, although her husband only nourishes her on worms an ell long and golden-yellow pie that he extracts from somewhere that it isn't polite to name.

"There's no longer anyone but you, and I'm finally seeing you, my dear daughter, my last consolation and the staff of my old age, by means of the ivory talisman that my son-in-law the green dog gave me...but are you happy?"

"You can see, my very dear father, that I'm a Queen, and I have everything I wish." And immediately, she took him into a magnificent apartment, the richest and most brilliant that any man born of woman could ever see.

"And where is your husband?"

"He's out there in the prairie with the hundred oxen of his guard, bundling up hay for our supper."

"What are you saying? Oh, I can see that in spite of all these beautiful riches, it's you who is unfortunate. You're bearing all alone the penalty for my pride and your mother's vanity..." And he had tears in his eyes.

Her Imperial Majesty the beautiful Hhouiphhouip was moved, and, suppressing a sigh, she disguised her emotion with a little smile, so charming that Amour could be heard flapping his wings in pleasure. "You'll taste it, Papa," she replied.

"Me! Even if I still had the teeth returned to me by the jelly of Flemish sheep, Prussian deer and English boar that my son-on-law the Great Yellow Wolf gave me...but he satanic confined-hens' milk that my son-in-law the Blue Cock gave me ha put everything back the way it was..."

And the poor fellow started recounting how he had gone astray, how he had found the hare with the pink collar, the white lamb with the tinkling bell, the white blackbird and the yellow-red-blue-green muskrat; how he had been taken to the home of his son-in-law the green dog; how, by mans of the ivory talisman he had been to the home of his son-on-law the great yellow wolf, who had rejuvenated him; how Houssihoussa had made dolls; how he had been to the home of his son-in-law the blue cock, who had made him two hundred years old; how, in order to reproportion himself with Houssihoussa, he had had to return things exactly to what they had been before; how the good Houssihoussa had become angry—and he concluded by telling he beautiful Hhouiphhouip that, even having no more teeth, she would see that he was not going to eat hay.

"Don't worry, Papa, and let my husband take care of it. I'll call him, for I'm the only one he permits to disturb his royal occupations.

And the Queen went on to an amethyst balcony that overlooked the prairie; the green she-monkeys handed her a fine loudhailer made of four unicorn-horns admirably joined together, into which she started shouting: "*Queti-queti-bêêêê!* Rakiskiakiah! My father has come! My father has come!"

And suddenly, a *bêhêhêhêhêêêê* was heard, so loud that it made the golden frames of all the windows tremble harmoniously and all the golden vessels in the palace resound, along with those throughout the city of Mêhêhê —which produced a very agreeable concert. That was like the signal for public rejoicing, for the arrival of the father of the Queen, His Excellency Seigneur Brancabanda.

Her Imperial Majesty the beautiful Hhouiphhouip said to her father: "Here comes the King my husband; I'll go receive him." At the same time she got up, and

183

ran to meet her august husband, His Imperial Two-horned Majesty King Bêhêhê, the richest and most handsome of the Red Sheep.

"Dear Sire," she said to him, "Seigneur Brancabanda, my illustrious father, who has taken the trouble to come to see us, has arrived in your sublime golden palace. Has Your Imperial Two-horned Majesty had a good haymaking? O Heaven! What beautiful hay! It's embalmed."

"Bêhê!"—that is the "parbleu" of all sheep, red, white or black—"let him be welcome! Here in my chariot is the wherewithal for a feast, *bêhêhêhêhêê*! Bonsoir, my Father! Let me embrace you!"

"Bonjour Your Two-horned Majesty, my son-in-law."

"Are you well, our dear Father?"

"So so! I've been young, then old, then rejuvenated, and now I'm old again."

"That's life, Father. And your wife, our worthy Mother?"

"She's desolate, alas, Your Imperial Two-Horned Majesty my son-in-law; she had reverted to three years old by means of the jelly of my son his Crunching Highness Seigneur Hihouhâh, Your Imperial Two-Horned Majesty's brother-in-law, and she made dolls, but my son-in-law His Crested Eminence Seigneur Cocodinq having given me, with good intentions, an accursed confined-hens' milk that had made me old for having drunk too much, I gave some to your mother, with the sole aim of returning her to the age of reason, but it made her as old again as she was before, and she's inconsolable, which made the good woman turn her back on me."

"There's no great harm in that, Father. I have something that re-rejuvenates when one has already been rejuvenated once; I'll get you some wolf-bladders, which are even more efficacious than my brother-in-law Duc Hihouhâh's jelly."

"Oh, you'll render life to me, Your Royal Two-Horned Majesty my son-in-law, and to the good Houssihoussa, your poor tender Mother, more than life, for in truth, in spite of her goodness, she makes me angry..."

During this conversation between the father-in-law and the son-in-law, the green monkeys garnished the beautiful ivory troughs in the dining room with hay, while others filled beautiful onyx mangers with bran, and an orangutan—the son of the Great Ape of the Woods and the daughter of the King of the Congo, whom he had surprised while she was hunting, and, in consequence, a Prince of the Blood among both the negroes and the apes, who would have his choice of being King of either nation, but in the meantime was the butler of the Queen of Mêhêhê, capital of the Red Sheep—came to say: "Her very young, very beautiful, very sage, very intelligent, very coquettish and very clement Majesty the august Queen Hhouiphhouip, sublime spouse of His Doubly Horned Imperial Majesty King Bêhêhê, is served."

"Let's go to the trough, Papa," said the beautiful Hhouiphhouip. That word did not please the fellow overmuch, and, perceiving in the palace courtyard two beautiful plump pigs, making a collection with purses around their necks, he thought: *A nice filet of those Messieurs would suit me much better!* But he dared not expose his thought, remembering what his daughter Hhûeip had said to him in a similar circumstance. He sat down, therefore, pulling a face, between the King and the Queen while the butler watered the hay with ouron.[23]

The seasoning is worthy of the dish! thought Brancabanda.

The King, who was a great philosopher, said to him: We're metempsychosists, Father, but I won't tell you that we eat nothing here that has been alive. The plants and seeds on which we nourish ourselves have a life, although much less perfect than that of animals; all beings are graduated from the slightest degree of sensibility to the most perfect, which in this kingdom, was annexed to my brothers the Red Sheep before the arrival of the beautiful Hhouiphhouip, your very dear daughter, my noble spouse, who surpasses in perfection all the Red Sheep that there are and ever will be in all lands and in every century; but it is by virtue of taste, and because of the warmth of the climate, which makes alkaline and putrefying substances contrary to us, whereas the acid of fruit and liqueurs is favorable to us, that we are not carnivores like my brothers-in-law, your noble sons-in-law, and their subjects. Taste, then, this fruit seasoned with ouron; it is the local bread, but we have, like all other nations, more delicate foodstuffs to eat with it."

At the same time the green monkeys uncovered the golden manger, in which, in addition to the bran, there

---

[23] This word does not exist in French in the precise form in which it is rendered here, and when the narrator is asked what it means by his young listener he explains that it is "a salty liquid known to the Greeks." If, as seems superficially apparent, it means urine, it is unclear why he is dissimulating; previously, he simply said "piss," derivatives of the verb *pisser* being much the same in both English and French. Readers will doubtless make up their own minds as to whether he might mean something else and, if so, what it might be.

were all kinds of delicious fruits: pomegranates, pineapples, oranges, Maltese melons, Sicilian pistachios, peaches, greengages the size of goose-eggs, Corinthian grapes each pip of which weighed a pound, figs as big as gourds, a hundred and fifty-six kinds of pears, apples like pumpkins and a thousand other kinds of fruits. Finally, at each end one saw two quinces as yellow as gold, which were only there for ornamentation, each of which was as fast as Georges d'Amboise.

That's all right! the visitor said to himself. Purely for shame he took a small pinch of hay, which he nibbled lightly, but, finding the taste of the tender grass agreeable, the flavor being very similar to fried mushrooms, he ate a good half a bushel. Afterwards, having perceived walnuts as large as the rim of a well, lying in an excellent green juice, he ate half of one, and then he set about swallowing a few hundred little Mirabelle plums, gilded and reddened, as large as hen's eggs, the flesh of which was exquisite; after which he threw himself upon excellent roasted chestnuts, still hot, a little larger than Jerusalem artichokes, which caused him to ask for something to drink.

Immediately, the green she-monkeys poured ouron into beautiful cups made from as single ruby, which made the liquid as ruby-tinted as Burgundy wine—which cheered up Brancabanda greatly, who had not drunk any for a long time, for one can give us excellent liqueurs such as the finest carcass water of the dog-fay, the topazed water of the snow-white ewes of the wolf-fay or the hen's-milked water of the cock-fay, but in drinking matters it is always necessary to come back to good wine; it is with that alone that a man rediscovers his heart. It was not the same, of course, since it was ouron, but it tasted similar.

The Great Bêhêhê put a certain very volatile essence in his glass and the Queen's the first time they drank.

"Dare I ask Your Two-Horned Imperil Majesty what that essence is?" Brancabanda asked

"It's wolf-bladder, my Father."

"Which you mentioned to me previously, and which re-rejuvenates?"

"Yes, Papa," said the beautiful Hhouiphhouip.

"Ah! Put a little in my Beaune wine, I beg you."

"There you are, Father."

"A little more?"

"That's enough for this time."

The guest drank his ouron, and found it superior to Nuits, Beaune, Côte-Rôtie, Contredieux, Migrène, Chablis etc.

The fruits, which he had not yet touched, tempted him thereafter, and he ate a great many, for he found them as delicious as all the stews in the world, even those make of carcasses by his son-in-law the green dog, those made with Flemish mutton, Prussian venison and English boar by his son-in-law the yellow wolf, and those made with worms an ell long, flies, cockchafers, woodlice and scarabs, and the gilded pies, of his son-in-law the blue cock; but he always came back to the roasted chestnuts, in order to have the occasion to drink the ouron with the essence of wolf-bladder.

When he had eaten all those excellent things, his daughter the Queen of Mêhêhê presented him with a mouthful of hay to clean his teeth. He took it, and found it even better than in the beginning, to such an extent that he asked for a rick to be placed in the manger of his bedroom for the night, which they did not fail to do.

As it was early, and, in accordance with the custom of hot countries, nightfall is the time for diversions, it was proposed to His Excellency Seigneur Brancabanda that they go to the theater, which he welcomed.

There were excellent actors in Mêhêhê; I shall say who they were in due course; there were also excellent and very respectable authors, for they were placed above the red sheep; they were humans, the only members of our species there were in the kingdom. There were other authors too, but a notch below them and of a different species; I shall also say who they were in due course.

The human authors for whom Bêhêhê had the highest consideration had composed epic poems, polite and natural histories, tragedies, comedies, books of physics and moral philosophy, etc. The principal ones were named:

The great Iratlove, whose tragedy *Hatmemo* was being performed that day. The foundation of the play was a well-known historical episode arrived from the Kingdom of Camels. It is necessary to know that the camel Hatmemo, under the pretext of reforming his homeland, but in truth to satisfy his ambition and lust, wanted to change its religion and mores, which he succeeded in doing means of crimes and massacres, but the devotion of a few donkeys, his subjects, whom he had the secret of rendering enthusiastic—for there is nothing as courageous and cruel as donkeys one they are enthused. That was the basis of the tragedy, which was regarded as a masterpiece.[24]

---

[24] Voltaire's tragedy *Le Fanatisme, ou Mahomet le prophète* (1741) was premièred in Lille and published with a title-page claiming that its place of publication was Amsterdam, because it was too controversial to be staged in Paris. It would be even

The immortal Aussuero, perhaps even greater, who had proved to his peers, apparently out of gratitude for the good treatment he had received from King Bêhêhê, that it was better to be a red sheep, or any other four-legged individual, than to be a human being.

The illustrious Funfbo, who, by virtue of views different from the immortal Aussuero, had written the history of all the inhabitants of the Earth, whether humans, apes, bears, dogs, lions, tigers, horses, donkeys, oxen, goats, sheep, pigs and even bats and rats, for which the yellow-red-blue-green muskrat had given him humble thanks; cocks, grouse, pheasants, eagles, vultures, all the way to the wren, for which the white blackbird had whistled him a very pretty song; all the fish, etc. but they had not complimented him for want to being able to talk; they had merely delegated a white bear or sea-marten on an ice-floe, which had made many beautiful things understood by means of sign-language; meanwhile, the beavers, who counted in the quality of amphibians, in order to be appointed ambassador of the aquatic population, apart from illicit favor, sent an individual deputation with lavish presents of furs and very warm thanks.

There were also works by deceased authors that were held in great veneration, such as the sublime Cornillat, of whom the entire nation of crows, who claimed descent from him, was very proud; the elegant and tender Riza, the model of fine language, an enchanter and painter; the penetrating flagellator of ridicules Podemoquelièlinre,[25] one of whose comedies was

more unthinkable to stage it there today, though not for the same reasons.
[25] This anagram combines Molière's stage name with his real name, Poquelin. Cornillat is, of course Corneille, Riza Racine

190

being performed that day with Iratlove's tragedy; the touching and instructive Lonféne, who had been a Pontiff without deceiving people, and who had published, for the instruction of kings, and amusing book appropriate to educate the whole world, etc., etc., etc.

The audience went into the spectacle at about ten o'clock, to emerge two hours after midnight. The tragedy was played superbly in certain roles; the actor who plated Hatmemo, named Niakel, carried off all suffrage; as for the green she-monkey who played a cameless, apart from being small, old and simpering, she wept with dry eyes. As for the green monkey Lavrebaud, who played the camel Raom, his walk zigzagged and his sniffling accent made Brancabanda laugh until he wept, which greatly scandalized the bears and other serious individuals who were in the audience. There was also a thin little sapajou name Éolm, who played the young camel, the brother of the young cameless Errympla, who uttered funny *hmm-hahs* while speaking, but Brancabanda did not laugh because he trembled in anticipation of the poor sapajou falling into a faint at any moment. As for the old monkey Darbriz, who was playing the role of the camel Eripoz, Hatmemo's enemy, the visitor found good points, but it was visible that his enthusiasm came in surges, like that of a forge, sometimes hot and sometimes extinguished by water poured on to it, and that the monkey in question, to whom nature had given the most venerable face that a monkey could have, only had a borrowed heat and light.

---

and Lonféne Fénelon. The names of the actors and actresses would not mean much today's readers even unscrambled, so I shall leave them unannotated.

Finally, the tragedy finished, and after a very tedious intermission, the comedy was performed, entitled *Misomelon*, or *The Enemy of the Red Sheep*—which is as if one said in French *The Misanthrope*. The subject of the play is a red sheep revolted by all the abuses he sees, who responds to them with too much bitterness, which is really an antisocial vice. The criticism of that admirable play is so fine, so delicate and so philosophical that the majority of the red sheep spectators, and all the quadruped spectators in general, sided with the misomelon, finding him virtuous—as if one could have any other virtue than that which renders a red sheep appropriate to live in society. The skillful and ingenious Podemoquelièlinre had also put into the play another honest red sheep, who was the veritable social sheep, whom ought to be taken for a model...

The role of the misomelon was played by a very good monkey, but very tall, and so close to the human that Brancabanda, who was deceived by that, made signs of intelligence to him, as to a member of his own species. It was even worse with regard the she-monkey, the mistress of the monkey misomelon; the fellow clapped his hands several times, and wanted to pay her a compliment after the performance, but was quite astonished to find no one behind the curtain but a rather disagreeable she-monkey.

After the two plays there was a ballet of rather pretty sapajous, in which two bears tried to dance, but did so very clumsily. Brancabanda noticed an extremely pretty young she-monkey who danced poorly but whose face everyone applauded; the poor child was so grateful that she made a great effort to jump, to the extent that she gave herself a sprain.

As Brancabanda could not stay in Mêhêhê for two whole days, the Opera had been postponed until the theater finished. That spectacle, which had just been entrusted to a new administration, was doubly interesting for Brancabanda. A new piece was being performed that day, which the Great Red Sheep had commissioned Iratlove to write, entitled *The Four Beauties and the Four Beasts*, and for which the human Clugk had composed the music. The piece was to be played by excellent actors of both sexes, and the King and Queen, were promising themselves an infinite pleasure therein. This is the subject.

In the first act the four beauties and their brothers were seen dancing in the courtyard of their house. Four ugly children and their sisters went past in the background, watching them with admiration. Then a little old woman arrived, who asked for the four beauties in marriage for the four ugly boys and offered the ugly girls for the brothers of the four beauties. The latter departed to go see the old woman's four daughters. They met the ugly boys, whom they mocked. They arrived at the old woman's house and, seeing monsters instead of young beauties, flew into such a great rage that they took them with them in order to leave them at the mercy of ogres in the middle of a wood.

Afterwards, amid frequent changes of scene, the ugly children were seen with their four animals, and asked for the four beauties in marriage. Then, at the blast of a whistle, the four brothers were seen again at the door of an ogre, who had them come in and tied them up like a bunch of asparagus; all the cries and plaints were in very fine music. The ballet was danced by young women as red as cherries and as white as lilies, and little boys destined to be eaten by the ogres, but who were rescued by the little old woman. The ballet would have been charming if the dancers executing it had put more feeling into it; they smiled at the ogre and pulled faces at their liberatrix. But what sublime talents the leading dancers were! What fire and energy there was in the movements of the stout Ralda (a word that signifies "winged" in Sheepish); what voluptuousness in those of Druimag! How Wlinhe excited admiration! How ravishing Validor and Nilessa were! Venus had lent them her girdle.

The Operadian leading dancers perhaps surpassed them again: Lauverdab gave Brancabanda such great pleasure by her gaiety that it lent powerful aid to the effect of the wolf-bladder; Sirvest astonished him; Elgrad pleased him; Merdacat seemed to him to be a light sylph. New as the visitor was to it all, he sensed the advantage one would be able to obtain from those great actors, who excelled in all genres, whether they were representing ogres, tender lovers or red sheep, etc.

That was the first act, in which Brancabanda was unable to recognize himself, because when it was a question of him, things were not complimentary to him, and he was ignorant of the rest.

In the second act, one saw an old man planting cabbages, and the four animals that came to abduct his daughters. The music expressed the different passions that had agitated the old man, his wife, his daughters, and the green dog, whose barking was rendered naturally by the song of a certain operadian monkey, named Élign in Sheepish; the yellow wolf, represented naively by the operadian Anurdad; the blue cock, whose piercing cock-a-doodle-doos were expressed by the admirable voice of the operadian Slorge; and the red sheep, to whom the operadian Élibrera lent enchanting graces and a regal majesty. The four beauties were represented, Hhûeip by the operadienne Nulpad, Hhûhhuip by the operadienne Lineubamé, Bizibizibizi by the operadienne Darunol—who, more unfortunate than the nymph Echo, survived her touching voice—and Hhouiphhouip by the pleasant operadienne Elasoir, who embellished harmony itself.

Hhûeip was seen to depart ugly and then, by virtue of a blast of the whistle, arrive in the land of the green dogs as beautiful as the day; she admired her ivory palace and visited all its apartments, having pretty girls for servants, who each had a little haze-skin neatly attached to the shoulder like a shoulder-knot.

After another blast of the whistle, the scene shifted to the land of the yellow wolves; then, another blast of the whistle and it was no longer that but a cage-city in which one was coiffed in plumes; the blue cock appeared with his wife, who had been carried away ugly but who was possessed of ravishing beauty. Like her sisters, she amused herself visiting its apartments and hearing the concerts of all the species of birds, which the orchestra executed admirably.

Brancabanda was delighted, when a whistle-blast came, with the most forceful illusion, to transport the scene to the land of the red sheep, which gave a great deal of pleasure to the entire audience.

In the third act, the four beauties, reunited, asked a fay to see their father and mother again. With a thrust of her magic wand, the fay formed a living tableau, in which everything that the worthy folk had in their home was seen. Brancabanda did not believe that it was him, but a parallel adventure, on seeing the old man and his wife sit down at table and weep instead of eating, saying:

Alas, our children!

Our poor children,
Have lost their life,
Stolen from them
In their best years!
Our dear children,
So lovely, so pleasant,
Our poor daughters,
Adroit and genteel,
Shall we ever hear your voices again?
There are our sons' places;
They are no more!
There are our daughters' places;
They are no more!
They are no more!
Etc.

In the fourth act, the old man came to visit the four beauties. Brancabanda laughed wholeheartedly on seeing the conduct of the poor fellow in the home of his daughters depicted naturally, and when he saw him fencing with the mirrors; he saw him become young, then old; his wife made dolls, which the actress Direxue rendered marvelously, because of the infantile sound of her voice.

At a blast of the whistle, everything changed, and something else appeared. Until then, the old man had been represented in the opera without Brancabanda recognizing himself for a particular reason. But what made him laugh imperiously was seeing the old man three years old again, in the home of the King with the ruby fleece, and then taken back to his wife, who had been rejuvenated and was dying of the desire to be a second time; singular things happened there, but so naturally that they gave great pleasure to the entire Court, and much honor to the human Iratlove.

Finally, the fifth act offered a pompous spectacle; a beautiful action was seen on the part of the wife of the infant-old man, which brought about the happiest denouement.

After leaving the Opera, the King and the Queen had a light snack. As for Brancabanda, he said that he was only thirsty; he asked for ouron and it was given to him.

Now, it is necessary to observe that, without being aware of it, Brancabanda had returned to the age of fifteen, thanks to the virtue of the wolf-bladder he had drunk. That had happened during the opera; while the ouron rejuvenated the body, the opera rejuvenated the mind, by virtue of a certain property of the spectacle—an effect perceived every day in Paris. Brancabanda, having become a veritable scatterbrain, observed where His Two-Horned Majesty put the wolf-bladder; he took the phial secretly, and to each cup of ouron that he drank, he added the essence, with neither discipline nor measure.

After the snack, it was a question of going to bed. The Queen wanted to take hr Papa personally to the apartment destined for him, which was all in gold, hung with crimson silk, obtained from red-gold worms that lived exclusively on gum instead of leaves. The green she-monkeys laid him down in a beautiful bed, which, although it was only red wool offered to the king in homage by young blood-red lambs at the end of infancy, was nevertheless so soft and comfortable that a flea leaping on to it would have left a footprint. Brancabandra sank into it and slept until broad daylight the following day, with Iouriri at his feet.

As soon as he woke up he started to laugh; a host of agreeable ideas presented themselves to his light imagi-

nation. He sat up and played with his curtains; everything amused him; he tried to pull Iouriri's ears, who
fled, guioring, to where his duty summoned him. A fly
went past in mid-air; he caught it, tied a thread round its
body and made it drag a wisp of straw.

While he was playing thus, the green she-monkeys,
chambermaids of Her Imperial Majesty the beautiful
Queen Hhouiphhouip, having heard bursts of laughter
and a voice saying: "Hey, hey, huro, dia, Fly!" they understood that he was awake and went into the room to
dress him. They dressed him as a hussar; his coat was
covered with gemstones; his turbaned hat, which was
surmounted by a beautiful petrified peacock's tail, of
which Prince Cocodinq had made a present to his sister-
in-law the Queen, displayed more riches than Peru and
Chile put together.

One thing that appeared to strike him slightly, but
only affected him momentarily, so light and superficial
was it, was that everything that was put on him seemed
to shrink by three-quarters. However, he played with the
green she-monkeys who were dressing him, and sometimes, without meaning any harm, played pranks at
which they blushed, laughing like lunatics. It was much
worse, however, when he saw the Queen; she seemed to
him to be as tall as a bell-tower; he could scarcely recognize her, and yet he did, because "good blood cannot
lie."

He had a terrible fear of His Two-Horned Imperial
Majesty the King of the Red Sheep, his son-in-law, who
appeared to him to be as big as an elephant; it was very
difficult to get him to accommodate himself to his presence, but they finally succeeded, and Brancabanda did
not take long to start playing in his silky red fleece. He
even climbed on to His Majesty, saying that he wanted a

ride, and the entire Court was in tears laughing on seeing the King serve as a mount to his father-in-law; but he was only more respectable for that in the eyes of his subjects, who still cite that example of filial piety to their children today.

While Brancabanda was riding around the palace like that on his royal mount, he reached the room where his son-in-law the red sheep granted audience to the ambassadors sent to him by neighboring Kings; the room was entirely garnished with angular mirrors, a present from the Prince of Coqueliquette, the Great Cocodinq, husband of the beautiful Bizibizibizi. It was very adroit politics on the part of Bêhêhê to give audiences in that room. The ambassadors were received at the entrance; the throne was in the middle, surrounded by Sheep of the Blood, and the hundred oxen of the King's guard, all well horned, filled the background—but instead of a hundred, the multiplying the mirrors made it appear that there were at least ten million; which gave ambassadors who were unfamiliar with the effect of the mirrors such a high opinion of the power of His Imperial Two-Horned Majesty the Great Red Sheep that their masters sent him presents every year in order to conserve his amity.

As soon as Brancabanda was in that room he began uttering cries of joy at the sight of a troop of magnificently-dressed small boys who were surrounding him. He got down rapidly from his royal mount and said that he wanted to go and play with the jolly little boys. The green monkeys, who had not quit him, tried to make him see reason, but there was no means of doing so; he wanted absolutely to play with the little boys. The King bleated until he was in tears. The Queen arrived and, touched by her dear father's error, spoke to him with so much tenderness and kindness, making him touch the mirrors with his fingers, that she convinced him, as much as an infant can be convinced, that it was his own image that he was seeing. Trying to awaken a useful pride, in order to excite him to virtue, she told him that when one is such a young and handsome child, it is necessary to be good.

Little Brancabanda—for he had become so by virtue of the immoderate use he had made, in secret, after the Opera, at the midnight snack, of his father-in-law the red sheep's essence of wolf-bladder—listened meekly to those remonstrations, made with tenderness and by a pretty mouth. He asked to leave the palace, and King Bêhêhê whistled for the muskrat Iouriri Yellow-red-blue-green, who brought the chariot to which the twelve thousand rats were harnessed.

That gave Brancabanda a great deal of pleasure; he started caressing them and kissing them, saying: "Pretty little Dadas! Pretty little Dadas!" He climbed into the vehicle with the King and the Queen, who put him on her knees, in order to take him to visit the capital, to see everything that was curious and show him to the people.

His Imperial and Two-Horned Majesty the red sheep, although he knew perfectly well that his father-in-law could not understand what he said to him, nevertheless explained everything, for the Prince knew that the traces imprinted in a child's brain remain there, although not understood, and that sooner or later they produce their fruit, good or bad according to the nature of the impressions.

In the first street that they traversed they found nothing but merchants. Now, in the great city of Mêhêhê, the capital of the red sheep, commerce is exercised by foxes with peacocks' tails; their wives have the body of a she-fox and the head of a hoopoe, and are very engaging; little Brancabanda found them very pretty and they gave him many caresses. The government had wanted them all to be on the same street, "because," said the Prime Minister, who was a very thoughtful hippopotamus also responsible for the departments of agriculture and the navy, "all the merchants thus brought together will make a single rich shop, furnished with everything that the citizens might desire."

At the end of that street there was another, entirely occupied by artisans, and each métier was ordinarily exercised by a single species of animal, whose houses were contiguous.

At the corner of the street of the merchants and that of the artisans there was a beautiful convent. The Queen, who was a little devout, wanted her father to see the Houhous. One of the hundred-oxen of the guard rang. A pig porter appeared.

"*Houhou, houhouhou!*" he said. "What do you want?"

"To see your house!" bellowed the hundred-ox.

"Houhou! The Fathers are occupied in the most important affair of life and it isn't possible to disturb them."

"*Sapoquemake!* It's very necessary that your Houhou be disturbed!"

"The Fathers are in the refectory."

"I who am ringing tell you that it is the Queen and her father, with the Sire His Majesty."

"*Houhou, houhouhou*, I'll go and inform the Father Prior then."

A Houhou weighing at least twenty-five thousand pounds came immediately and, suppressing the *houhous* of his speech, delivered a find harangue to Brancabanda, who, while he grunted the most beautiful things in the world, amused himself pulling out his silks. Then the porcine prior begged the King and Queen to give the holy house the pleasure and the honor of offering them dinner.

"But you've just dined, Reverend," said the beautiful Hhouiphhouip.

"We'll recommence, Madame, in order to have the honor of eating in the presence of Your August Majesty, for it's in the difficulty that we have in stuffing the stomach that our greatest mortification consists."

As it was the hour when they had breakfast at Court, Their Majesties accepted. They went into a vast hall ten thousand nine hundred and eighty feet long, furnished with four rows of golden tables that extended over its entire length.

"This is our refectory, Madame, which is also our common room," said the porcine prior to the Queen.

Their Majesties sat down, and little Brancabanda, who was on the Queen's knees, started shouting, on seeing the Houhous eating: "I'm hungry!"

Immediately, the table was covered with all sorts of dishes; the Houhous regarnished theirs and recommenced chewing, as if they had not eaten anything for a fortnight.

"See their zeal," said the porcine prior. "They're expressing it to Your Majesties in the most vivid fashion, and even if they have an indigestion, they won't rest until all the plates are cleared!"

The King praised the marks of respect that were being shown to him, and his Two-Horned Majesty presented a few fruits to the Queen, who made Brancabanda eat them. Then, having testified a desire to taste the Reverends' soup, she found that it was puréed fat. As she did not have the same ideas of mortification as the inhabitants of the kingdom of the red sheep, she asked the porcine prior why that was, and he replied very sagely:

"Madame, meat being unhealthy in the climate of the superb city of Mêhêhê, we eat as much of it as possible, in order to mortify ourselves."

The Queen was greatly edified by that response, and felt a great deal of compassion for the good Houhous, two whom the King wanted to testify his satisfaction with a considerable present of acorns and barley—but they begged His Two-Horned Majesty to give it to them in gold, and, in order that they would not violate their vow of poverty, to send it to them in a large barrel, along with iron tongs, of which the porcine treasurer would make use in order to take out the gold without touching it. Such delicacy charmed the Queen even more, who, being naturally pious, was very pleased with those holy personages, even though their exterior was a little unpleasant.

Then, a dish of a very common vegetable was served to the porcine prior, the procurer and the other principal officers, who practiced an authority sterner than the ordinary Houhous.

"Ah!" said the King, laughing "That's against the rule!"

The Queen, still out of devotion, wanted to taste it; she found that they were cocks' kidneys, deliciously seasoned, and, remembering the holy motive, she only held them in higher esteem.

"They are, Madame," the porcine prior told her, "the kidneys of the roast chickens that we make our poor brothers at every Friday at lunch, who perform that act of mortification with an edifying resignation.

In order to sanctify her dear father, little Brancabanda, Her Majesty made him eat a little plate of those kidneys, and the little fellow, after having finished every last one, shouted at the top of his voice: "More! I want more! More bonbons!" As the dish was light, he was satisfied, until he was full—which was, the Houhous remarked to the Queen, a sign of predestination.

When little Brancabanda had eaten well they left the holy house in order to go into the street of goldsmiths. It was horses that exercised that fine métier, of indispensable necessity in Mêhêhê, where everything, including the roofs of the houses, is made of gold. They saw pretty and spirited fillies in the shops, well-dressed, with beautiful horse-cloths and plumes.

Continuing their route, they reached the street of the donkeys. That species had been much degraded for several generations, for a reason to be mentioned; nowadays they were all simply millers; the oxen were laborers, the camels porters. Billy-goats were scorned because they had once disputed the empire with the red sheep; the latter, having got the upper hand, had constrained them to follow the métiers of tanners, curriers, leather-dressers, shoemakers, and even to exercise the trade known in Spain as *Çapatero-in-viejo*;[26] but nanny-goats, out of consideration for their sex, were gardeners and florists. Beavers were masons, roofers, carpenters and hatmakers.

Elephants were judges; the procurator general was a rhinoceros, the interrogator a tiger, the executioner a leopard, jailers bulldogs, court clerks cats, prosecutors hyenas, advocates mongrels, ushers rattlesnakes, notaries rabbits and notaries' clerks hares.

---

[26] i.e. *zapatero de viejo*, or cobbler.

Bears were printers, rent-collectors and tax-collectors; and moles were librarians.

Birds were messengers; tawny owls and barn owls were night-watchmen; polecats, weasels, ferrets and all of their kin were rag-pickers, gutter-sweepers, lantern-bearers, hawkers of old hats, toilet attendants, spies, etc.

The kingdom's troops were made up of a general staff of lions, who had under their orders barbets, mastiffs and several regiments of battle-hardened bulls; wolves formed the light infantry.

Monkeys exercised six different professions on their own; they were second-rate authors—those of the first class being humans, that beautiful art only being exercised in its perfection by the kings of nature—actors, painters, sculptors, musicians (in which four professions there was a human or two in each in the whole kingdom) and tailors (in that one there were only monkeys).

She-monkeys were fashion-merchants, chamber-maids, maidservants, cooks and laundresses, not to mention that they could also be actresses, either at Mêhêhê's three theaters, the Sheepish, the Simian and the Opera, or among the strolling players of fairgrounds.

As for rats, who are highly esteemed among the red sheep, among whom they are similar to dogs among humans, they have a good lot; they are charged with governing all heads, and they also serve as horses to the King and Queen, much like the Swiss in the Park of Versailles, under the direction of the Great Muskrat Iouriri Yellow-red-blue-green.

Mice are responsible for cleanliness, and they are the ones who sweep the streets in the mornings before the round of the local Ape-Commissaire, for it is another species of large monkeys, very malign, who exercise that function.

The sapajous and other little monkeys with dog-like heads known as guenons, were hair-dressers and wig-makers.

The Houhous who had not been deemed worthy of admission to the holy house lived on the exercise of a profession that only operates in Paris after ten o'clock in the evenings, when all noses are closed.[27]

Certain privileged donkeys, because of their stoutness and the length of their ears, endowed with a very strong voice, were criers and schoolmasters, some were even Doctors of Absurdology.

As for physicians, that noble profession, once the lot of donkeys before they became millers, was no longer exercises except by read sheep, Princes of the Blood. The former Kings ancestors of His Two-Horned Majesty, had established that law for reasons of sage politics. It is necessary to know that previously, the red sheep heir to the throne either had his brother princes murdered, blinded or abelarded. The people were horrified by that barbarity, and were on the point of revolt several times.

Bêhêhê XCIX, cleverer than his ancestors, issued an edict in which he declared that in future, no Prince of the Blood would be put to death. The capital immediately resounded with cries of joy and benedictions.

A week later he issued a second edict, which ordered that every physician who had not saved his patient would be buried with him. The Prince was blessed again and immediately, all the onagers quit the ermine, the red robe and the square bonnet.

---

[27] i.e. cesspit-emptiers.

Finally, a week after that, a third edict was issued, "registered at the Parliament of Elephants and moved by the King's Rhinoceros-General, to be executed in accordance with its form and tenor, without any modifications," by which His Two-Horned Majesty, "touched by paternal love for his subjects, in view of the extreme importance of the profession of medicine, previously abandoned to onagers who were unworthy of exercising it," ordered that in future, medicine would only be practiced by Princes of his Red Sheep Blood.

By means of the second edict, however, which was rigorously observed, no Princes of the Blood ever remained except those from whom the King had nothing to fear, by which one can see how admirably sagacious the red sheep are.

There were also in Mêhêhê a few monasteries of Houhoues, but as males of any species could not enter them, the King and Queen passed them by.

After little Brancabanda had had a good excursion, they went back to the palace for dinner at about four o'clock. They ate hay, pineapples, pomegranates, melons, oranges, apricots, peaches, greengages the size of goose-eggs, a hundred and fifty-six kinds of pears, Corinthian grapes each pip of which weighed a pound, figs as big as gourds and a thousand other species of fruits. Little Brancabanda wanted to taste the quinces as big as Georges d'Amboise, but the Queen told him that he was being a baby. Then they ate walnuts the size of well-heads and roasted chestnuts as big as Jerusalem artichokes, which made them drink a lot, but without any wolf-bladder—for the King and Queen only put it in their beverage once a month, and precisely the quantity necessary to repair the aging to which they had been subject since the last dose. They drank from cups made of a single ruby, which gave the liquid therein the color of Burgundy wine.

After dinner, there was a question of little Brancabanda's departure, in the cool of the evening, in his chariot drawn by twelve thousand muskrats, guided by Iouriri Yellow-red-blue-green; for he could not stay any longer because of the good Houssihoussa, who would be dying of impatience at not receiving the wherewithal to re-rejuvenate herself.

Before then, however, His Two-Horned Majesty the King of the Red Sheep performed the customary daily ceremony to make abundance reign in his Estates. It is necessary to say that above the great dining-room there was a vast storehouse, in which the peel of all the orang- es, lemons, limes, etc. that were consumed every year throughout the kingdom was put to dry. It was the eq- uine goldsmiths who were charged with storing it, after which it was collected and put in piles by dormice, sin- gularly adept at amassing it, as well as broken bottles. Now, as soon as the peel had received the influence of His Red Sheep Majesty's expiration, it changed, that of the oranges into gold coins of the value of a French dou- ble-louis, and that of lemons into silver coins of the val- ue of a six-livre écu. That was the national currency.

There was, however, only His Two-Horned Majesty who could extract it from the warehouse. Every day, therefore, after dinner, Bêhêhê had a ladder made of ar- omatic wood brought and climbed up it; and when His Imperial Two-Horned Majesty's head was within range of a large golden joist in which there was a hole like those in trunks or money-boxes, he bumped it in the fashion of a ram, and at each thrust of his forehead and royal horns, a millions gold coins fell, and four million silver coins, as many as there were of metamorphosed pieces of peel. Thus Bêhêhê furnished currency to his three brothers-in-law.

It was that beautiful operation that His Majesty the Great Red Sheep, husband of the beautiful Hhouiphhouip, allowed his father-in-law to see, which amused him greatly; he even wanted to go up to bump his own head but his daughter the Queen made him understand that he would hurt himself, his forehead not being as hard, and that, in any case, it was necessary to go.

Child as he was, little Brancabanda did not fail to say, by virtue of reminiscence: "Oh what a fine fellow the King is! What a pity that such an honest fellow is only a sheep!"

"Father," replied the Red Sheep, "When candor and piety withdrew from humans, they took refuge among us."

The child, who had spoken mechanically, like an intelligent Parisian three-year-old, made no response.

There was a whistle, and that sage, discreet and laconic individual Iouriri, the great yellow-red-blue-green muskrat, who had been to fetch Brancabanda, was instructed to take him back; to give the Queen's mother, the good Houssihoussa, the essence of wolf-bladder; to inform her as to the manner of making use of it; and to explain everything regarding the infant Brancabanda, her husband. The golden chariot having been laden with all sorts of fruits and bottles of ouron, fine garments for Houssihoussa and a large quantity of gold and silver coins to serve as counters when Brancabanda and his wife played the noble game, recovered from the Greeks, of Oie,[28] or Brisquenbille, little Brancabanda was put into it. He kissed the Queen, calling her Maman, and, charmed by his little Dadas, was eager to see them set off. A happy age!

The Queen, moved to tears, her heart oppressed, embraced her dear father for the last time; Iouriri cracked his whip, and the chariot flew.

They arrived the following day at eight o'clock in the morning at the house of the good Houssihoussa. She had only just woken up, because she had spent a sleepless night, very anxious because Brancabanda had not returned. As soon as she perceived the chariot she was transported by joy, not doubting that her husband was bringing back the wherewithal to rejuvenate herself. She searched for him with her eyes, and, discovering behind the yellow-red-blue-green muskrat a pretty little child. she mistook him for an Amour that her son-in-law the red sheep had sent her to bring up at the spit.

"Handsome little Cupid," she said to him, "be welcome!"

Little Brancabanda, seeing a woman tanned by the sun, thin, toothless and wearing a negligee—a rather neglected negligee—was afraid and pushed her away, crating: "I want to go back to my beautiful Maman; I don't want this nasty old woman!"

---

[28] The *jeu d'Oie* [the Goose Game] is a board game in which the players' counters follow a spiral track of 63 spaces, as dictated by throws of a die, spaces marked with a goose permitting the player another roll, and some being equipped with short-cut bridges. It is the ancestor of Ludo, Snakes & Ladders, etc. Its speculative association with ancient Greece, based on a Minoan clay disk with a spiral design, is probably mistaken.

"Madame," the muskrat said, then, "the Great Monarch, the Two-Horned Majesty who governs with a golden scepter the vast and powerful kingdom of the Red Sheep, the husband of the beautiful and superlicquencious Princess the beautiful Hhouiphhouip, the youngest and the best, as well as the most honorifically married of Your Excellency's daughters, who lives in her crystal palace roofed with rubies, in the magnificent and most architecturally built of cities, the city of Mêhêhê, where the houses are agate and roofed in gold; where foxes with peacocks' tails are merchants, where she-foxes have hoopoes' heads; where a hippopotamus is the prime minister, where a hundred oxen are Swiss guards; where pigs are monks, where sows are nuns, where horses are goldsmiths and their spirited mares well-ornamented by horse-cloths and plumes serve as marvelous salespersons; where donkeys, formerly physicians, are millers, oxen common laborers, camels porters, billy-goats, former rebels, tanners, curriers, leather-dressers, shoemakers and cobblers and their wives the nanny-goats gardeners and florists, beavers masons, roofers, carpenters and hat-makers; where elephants are judges, rhinoceroses public prosecutors, tigers interrogators, leopards executioners, bulldogs jailers, cats court clerks, hyenas prosecutors, mongrels advocates, rattlesnakes bailiffs, rabbits notaries and hares errand-boys; where bears are printers, rent-collectors and tax-collectors and moles librarians; where birds are messengers, owls night-watchmen, martens, weasels and ferrets hawkers of old hats, rag-pickers, gutter-sweepers, lantern-bearers, lavatory attendants and spies; where the troops are composed of lions, barbets, mastiffs, bulls and lupine light infantry; where monkeys are authors, actors, painters, sculptors, musicians and tailors; where she-monkeys are fashion-merchants, chambermaids, maid-servants, laundresses, cooks, actresses and dancers, even at the Opera; where rats, like your servant, have the government of all heads and have the honor of ferrying the King and the Queen; where mice are street-sweepers; where apes are commissaires; where tailed monkeys are hairdressers and wig-makers; where pigs devoid of monastic habits follow a profession that makes everyone hold their noses; where certain donkeys, because of the length of their ears are criers, schoolmasters and even Doctors of Absurdology; where medicine, once practiced by onagers, is today practiced by Princes of the Red Sheep Blood, who are buried with their patients—in a word, Madame, the Great Bêhêhêhêêêê, Your Excellency's son-in-law, has sent me here, as the most discreet and laconic of his ministers, to compliment you and to bring back to you His Excellency your noble husband, in this golden chariot, harnessed to twelve thousand yellow-red-blue-green muskrats and laden with presents of fruits as well as gold and silver coins, which will serve as counters when you play with His Excellency the Noble Seigneur Monseigneur de Brancabanda the noble game recovered from the Greeks of Oie or Brisquenbille.

"You should know, noble lady," the muskrat continued, "that the King my Master has the essence of wolf-bladder that rejuvenates when one has already been rejuvenated, by putting a drop into a glass of ouron, a few jars of which I have brought Your Excellency, of which ouron and which essence of wolf-bladder your illustrious husband the noble Seigneur Brancabanda used too much in secret at the midnight feast when His Excellency had come back from the Sheepish Theater where the tragedy of the human author Iratlove entitled *Hatmemo* and the comedy of the human author

Podemoquelièlinre entitled *Misomelon* had been performed—for Your Excellency ought to know that we
have two sorts of authors, human authors and monkey
authors—and the Opera, where a piece in five acts had
been performed in which you, him, them, us and me all
had roles; with the consequence that it was a depiction of
everything that has happened and everything that...but
I'm saying too much...that's not because I'm loqua-
cious...but it's because...where was I?

"Oh, I know, I know: the ouron and the wolf's
bladder, of which His Excellency Seigneur Brancabanda,
your husband, used so much of it in secret at the midnight or early-morning snack on the evening of his arrival in the beautiful city of Mêhêhê, built of agate and
roofed in gold, in the crystal palace roofed in rubies of
the great Bêhêhêhêêêê, your son-in-law, husband of the
beautiful Hhouiphhouip, your daughter—who is marvelously well and embraces you with all her august heart—
that he as entirely re-rejuvenated, the proof of which you
have before your eyes; for this charming little child, who
has just called you a nasty old woman, is the noble and
illustrious Seigneur Brancabanda, your worthy spouse,
whom I am leaving you, with these presents of hay,
pineapples, pomegranates, oranges, Maltese melons,
apricots, peaches, pistachios, greengages as big as
goose-eggs, a hundred and fifty-six sorts of pears, Corinthian grapes each pip of which weighs a pound, figs like
gourds, apples like pumpkins, with walnuts like well-
heads and roast chestnuts and big as Jerusalem artichokes, not to mention the gold and silver coins, and
especially this phial of wolf-bladder essence, which
Your Excellency may use at her whim, following the
rules of extreme prudence, and thinking nevertheless that
Your Excellency cannot advance the age of her illustri-

ous husband without diminishing that of the very august Houssihoussa; for every spoonful of confined-hens' milk that you give him, it's necessary that Your Excellency swallow one of ouron with essence of wolf-bladder; but that will not be reciprocal and Your Excellency can re-rejuvenate herself alone as much as she wishes—which is to say, without re-aging the noble Seigneur Brancabanda."

The great and laconic muskrat Iouriri Yellow-red-blue-green, having thus guiored, stopped, out of breath, climbed back on to his chariot, saluted Houssihoussa with three profound inclinations, putting his head between his front legs, and departed, a hundred million times faster than he had talked.

When the good woman found herself mistress of the phial of essence of wolf-bladder and the jars of ouron, she was transported with joy. Looking at Brancabanda, who was rolling a little chariot that the Queen of the Red Sheep had given him, with which to amuse himself during the journey, she said to him: "Ah, my little fellow, you're going pay me back for everything you have had from me during your life; keep a straight course or you'll see a fine to-do. Well, here I am, mistress of my re-rejuvenation—but is it necessary to start right away, since I have no one to please? Let's enjoy my authority over Monsieur my husband a little. Come on, little boy, on your knees, beg pardon for what you said when you arrived...."

Little Brancabanda stated to cry; the good woman got angry; the little fellow redoubled his cries; the good woman whipped him, whipped him and whipped him until she was weary, and then put him to bed without supper.

"Oh, you'll grow up again," she said to him, "but that will take years."

Thus triumphed the good Houssihoussa, her husband's mistress.

However, she looked from time to time at the phial of wolf-bladder; then she remembered the shard of mirror-glass than her husband had brought from the house of his on-in-law the cock; she went to look for it and looked at herself in it; she frightened herself.

"What harm would it do me to return myself to twenty years of age, since I can re-rejuvenate myself without re-aging this brat? I was so good-looking at that age—all the boys followed me; one said: "What a nice figure she has!" another "How pretty she is!" another "What lovely eyes!" another "What beautiful hair!" another "What a pretty laugh!" another "What lovely hands!" another "How spick and span she is!" another "How everything suits her!" and others even more agreeable things, which I only understood later... To see myself again as I was! Oh, how I could profit from my second youth! Who would have thought it? Come on, let's re-rejuvenate ourselves once and for all, and give us back our twenty years, no fewer. I'll still be mistress enough of his baboon, and I'll have time enough to make a man of him, if I wish, while remaining a young woman..."

So, Madame Houssihoussa started her supper with delicious fruits; then she ate a few chestnuts, which she found roasted; and then she was thirsty. She poured herself a glass of ouron, in which she mixed a little wolf-bladder, without measuring it very carefully.

As soon as she had drunk, she looked at herself, and saw herself visibly re-rejuvenating; youth stirred, stirred and stirred. As an east wind at daybreak clears the azure of a beautiful sky and chases away nebulous vapors, leaving nothing but light clouds that come to gild the brilliant harbinger of the day, so youth chased away the wrinkles and substituted for the livid and somber complexion of old age the lilies and roses of adolescence. Ecstatic with pleasure, Houssihoussa followed the renaissance of hr charms step by step.

"More…more… a little more!" she said.

Finally, the wolf-bladder fixed her between sixteen and seventeen years of age: a charming age at which reason illuminates with its divine flame without the naivety of childhood having yet deteriorated.

"There I am again!" she exclaimed, "Let's go to bed now; perhaps a good night's sleep will add even more to my freshness…"

And she went to bed—but could she sleep? Her heart was palpitating, and one cannot sleep when one's heart is palpitating. It is not that she often made the sad refection that there was no one there who could see her beauty—but at the age she was, after all, one likes to be beautiful unintentionally.

As dawn approached, she became drowsy for a few minutes; and then a dream came to trouble that moment of repose.

She thought she saw, in a charming meadow scattered with flowers, a handsome young man who was picking narcissi. As soon as she had perceived him, she fled, expecting him to follow her, but in vain; he was so young that he did not know as yet the price of beauty; he stayed there, preferring a feeble image to the reality. Chagrin woke the beauty up; she got up immediately in order to go look at herself. How beautiful she was!

After getting dressed, she thought about little Brancabanda, who was in his cradle, and whom she had put to bed without supper, after having whipped him soundly. She went to see him, and was astonished that she could have been so cruel.[29]

The child was asleep, candor and innocence reigned over his handsome face, and his tranquil young soul left his features all their regularity.

"How beautiful he is!" exclaimed the lovely Houssihoussa. "And he isn't five years old! We won't be able to converse reasonably, like two grown-ups. Oh, I've been very foolish, not to have advanced his age by giving him hen's milk while I was taking the wolf-bladder!"

Now, since Houssihoussa was sixteen years old, she was no longer so prudent; the desire to retain a husband in the cradle in order to govern him, does not enter such a young head, although it seems good at twenty-five, thirty, forty years and beyond. She kissed the child on the mouth, who woke up, and, seeing a young and pretty woman who resembled the beautiful Hhouiphhouip, Queen of the Red Sheep, hugging him in her arms and kissing him fondly, asked her joyfully for his little Dadas, and whether they were going to have breakfast with the Houhous, in order to eat bonbons there.

"No, my handsome love," the young Houssihoussa replied, giving him a thousand caresses, "but I'm going to give you everything you wish. At the same time she

---

[29] There is a brief interruption at this point in the original text, in which the listener express satisfaction at that contrition, which the narrator explains in terms of the alleged natural virtue of sixteen-year-old girls; but the note also contains the observation that "it has been necessary to change the ending of the tale completely, the details of which would have been insupportable by Parisian ears."

dressed him in his beautiful hussar costume, his fine tur-baned hat made in Coqueliquette by the hands of the lovely Tosirap, the most amiable of furriers, and when he was thus adorned, he was so very charming that Houssihoussa lavished him with caresses.

Little Brancabanda found that all well and good, but he was hungry and asked for bonbons like those in the house of the Houhous. Houssihoussa gave him hay, and he threw it in her face; she chose the most delicious fruits for him, but he would not touch them; she present-ed him with half of a quarter of a walnut swimming in excellent grape-juice, but the child started to cry, saying: "I want to go to the Houhous' house, where there are much better bonbons..."

Desolate, and as sensitive as a girl of sixteen, Houssihoussa did not know to which saint to appeal. *It's necessary to render him more reasonable*, she said to herself. *Yes, but I'd return to the cradle! For it's neces-sary for me to re-rejuvenate myself for as many years as I age him. That means that by aging him by...ten years...he'll be thirteen and I...I'd only be a snotty brat!*

She would not have said so the previous day, but if at forty-five one thinks one can never be too young, it is not the same at sixteen; one likes to remain grown up—it is such a great advantage. So, Houssihoussa did not want to go any further back.

"Let him cry as much as he wants," she said. And she held to that proposition.

She was right. When he had cried enough, Brancabanda shut up. His wife had put away the fruits; he only found the hay; and the little fellow, tormented by hunger, was happy to eat it, and stuff himself with it.

Houssihoussa, however, had good reasons for not persisting in her resolution; a girl so young and so beautiful, alone in a house in the middle of the woods, in the vicinity of ogres who had eaten Sacripar, Fandipouf, Farôdor and Craquoman, was at great risk. Add to that, that she was very timid. In spite of everything, though, terror could not do anything to engage her to re-age her husband and reduce herself below the most charming of ages; that would doubtless have been even worse than if it had been a question of becoming older herself. Finally, the concern for her subsistence, which would soon become disquieting, also made no impression on her.

I want to remain sixteen, she said to herself, *even if I die of hunger thereat.*

Any woman fifty years old, especially in Paris, would say the same, for there is nothing that women would not sacrifice to the desire to be young and beautiful—a desire always legitimate, with regard to the latter point, when it is understood. The desire to command, powerful as it is, in spite of the judgment of Queen Berthe related by Voltaire,[30] chief clerk of Paphos, yields to that powerful desire; but there is another sentiment that balances it and prevails, if not always, then at intervals, and that is the tender penchant of the heart.

Houssihoussa, young and beautiful, felt that she was made to love, and wanted to be loved. That did not happen in a day, but gradually. The beauty even had a spur more pressing than other young women; the latter are only guided by a blind instinct, but Houssihoussa also had an agreeable memory.

One day, when it was hot, she felt drowsy after dinner and fell asleep. An agreeable dream, as young as her, poured a delightful languor into her senses. In the mean-

---

[30] In the satirical poem "Ce qui plait aux dames" [What Pleases Ladies] (1764).

time, little Brancabanda was playing at her feet; without thinking about it, he took off a pretty slipper—for Queen Hhouiphhouip had sent Houssihoussa magnificent clothes, and attire suitable for a pretty and coquettish young woman, foreseeing that her dear mother would not fail to re-rejuvenate herself—and tickled the sole of a dainty foot gently; he touched her pretty leg, still un-thinkingly...

A child who is playing without thinking about it can go a long way...

Houssihoussa, troubled, raised her eyelids slightly,

"Charming...child.," she said, half dreaming. "Leave...leave...leave...then!"

The little rogue was still teasing, without thinking about it.

The beauty suddenly woke up.

"Oh!" she said. "Let's age him, since it's necessary; what will be, will be..."

She got up precipitately, ran to the chest that contained the confined-hens' milk, dazedly put all that remained into a glass of pure water and gave it to little Brancabanda to wallow.

The child found the liquor excellent. "More?" he said. "More, Maman? More..."

Houssihoussa waited for the hen's milk to take effect, but nothing happened.

"Alas," she said to herself, sighing, "it's necessary, then, to become a little girl again!" With that, she poured herself half a glass of ouron, threw into it, turning her eyes away, the rest of the wolf-bladder, and drank it, trembling. Amour, imperious Amour, sustained the glass, lifting it with the tip of his arrow, in order that she would drunk it to the last drop.

Scarcely had the liquid been swallowed than Brancabanda grew visibly in size. He reached the age of sixteen, where he stopped; at the same time, Houssihoussa shank, and was fixed again at an age between three and four years.

At that new age, Brancabanda knew himself, and remembered what he was; he had all the vivacity of youth, but he did not have the imprudence, and if he committed a few faults, they came from his mind, not the heart. He understood how the new metamorphosis had been operated, although he did not know exactly what motive the beautiful Houssihoussa had had—a motive to which one can add that small causes can have great effects, for kingdoms have often been overturned and half the world ravaged because women have wanted what young Houssihoussa wanted in reenlarging her husband.

To tell the truth, Brancabanda thought that his wife had sensed the beautiful verity that a man is the protector of his wife, her support and her defender, and that she had of her own accord and at her own expense wanted to put herself back in her place; he was very grateful for that. He resolved to form his young wife, from infancy, and to correct her character so completely of all the imperfections that had troubled their union that they would one day be in perfect accord.

He was right; all marriages would be happy if every husband could bring up his future wife.

After a few months, all the provisions that Brancabanda had brought from the home of his son-in-law the red sheep having been exhausted, he was in an embarrassing situation, for a great misfortune had occurred; the ivory talisman given to him by his son-in-law the green dog had been lost during his infancy. He still had a lot of gold, but it was not in current coinage, and it was a futile possession in a canton where there was no longer anything to buy, or to sell, since the surrounding area was deserted and no one wanted to have any commerce with the inhabitants of Charmelieu.

"Parbleu!" young Brancabanda said, one morning. "I'm being stupid not to profit from the lesson that my sons-in-law have given me. There must be carcasses in the vicinity; I'll go in search of them; I'll boil them; the flesh will make an excellent stew, which will become anything I want under my teeth, and the bones will change into ivory, of which I can build a palace like my son-in-law the dog.

So Brancabanda found a fine carcass, so large that it frightened little Houssihoussa; he put part of it in a cooking-pot, but the more he boiled it the less flesh there was and the more unbearable the odor became; he tried to sample it, but it was a poisonous stew, and the bones were good for nothing, except for the ribs, of which one might have made handles for two-sou knives.

Seeing that it was a waste of effort, Brancabanda said to himself: *It's necessary not to be discouraged by one thing that didn't succeed. My son-in-law the wolf had a less facile but more reliable secret; let's try to capture a sheep from one of the nearby sheepfolds.*

And he went to spy on the sheep of the shepherds of the nearest inhabited areas, such as Joux, Vermenton, Arci and Santepallaie Luci—but every time, the dogs nipped his buttock in a fine manner; once, he was nearly killed by a musket-shot fired at him by the shepherd of Luci-le-bois.

Let's see, said Brancabanda then, *whether the secret of my on-in-law the cock will succeed for me.* He searched for worms, but the stoutest of them were reduced by the fire to the width of a thread. Then he tried to make a pie...and the result was so unfortunate that the mephitic exhalations nearly suffocated him and little Houssihoussa.

Finally, Brancabanda gathered hay, which only smelled like grass, but he expected that. He did not even have the curiosity to beat his head against a wooden beam to see whether he could obtain something as useless as gold.

What could he do? Brancabanda finally took the course of action that he should have followed from the start; he was young and strong; he dug his garden, planted seeds that he had fortunately conserved, and succeeded in extracting a meager but adequate subsistence.

He lived thus for eight years. After work, he amused himself with little Houssihoussa, who was gradually growing up and becoming charming. A tender intelligence reigned between them. The hope of a happy future, as pleasant as the happiness itself, spread a salutary balm in their blood; they owed it to the fact that they possessed nothing superfluous, but also that nothing absolutely necessary was lacking to them; they were happy.

Houssihoussa had reached the age of twelve; Brancabanda was within sight of the keenly desired moment, when, one morning when it rained and he could not work in the garden, he started reminding his young wife of all their adventures. Houssihoussa listened with a curious attention.

When he reached the point at which his son-in law the King of the Red Sheep had bumped his head against a wooden beam in order to make gold and silver coins fall from the loft in which the orange and lemon peel were stored, Houssihoussa said to him: "My little husband, we have orange and lemon peel upstairs—there's a ladder, there's a joist, there's a hole; climb up and bump a little, in order to see..."

Brancabanda, who knew the futility of all his attempts, started to laugh, but amour rendered him obliging; he wanted to satisfy his little wife's curiosity. So he climbed the ladder, bumped his head against the joist, and saw fall down, not gold and silver coins, but the ivory talisman, which had been on the upper edge of the joist.

Transported with joy, Brancabanda got down rapidly; he explained to his wife what the talisman was, which could allow them to see once again their daughter Hhûeip and their son-in-law the green dog, whose palace was made of ivory; their daughter Hhûhhuip and their son-in-law the yellow wolf, whose palace was made of ebony; their daughter Bizibizibizi and their son-in-law the blue cock, whose palace-cage was made of gold and silver wire; and their daughter Hhouiphhouip and their son-in-law the red sheep, whose palace was made of crystal, roofed with rubies.

Houssihoussa was charmed by that fortunate find and begged her husband not to put off for a moment the desired arrival of all the chariots. Immediately, Brancabanda took his talisman and, giving himself a grave expression that made little Houssihoussa laugh like a lunatic, he started to say: "By the nose of the Marquis my son-in-law His Mordant Highness the Green Dog, may his chariot be here, harnessed to roe deer, conducted by the hare with the pink collar. By the tooth of the Duc my son-in-law His Crunching Highness the Great Yellow Wolf, may his chariot be here, harnessed to white sheep, conducted by the lamb with the tinkling bell. By the crest of the Prince my son-in-law His Crested Eminence the Great Blue Cock, may his chariot-cage be here, harnessed to storks, cranes and wild geese, conducted by the white blackbird. By the horn of the King my son-in-law His Two-Horned Majesty the Great Red Sheep, may his chariot be here, harnessed to twelve thousand muskrats, conducted by the laconic orator Iouriri Yellow-red-blue-green, who changes them into a whale when he wishes by rubbing their muzzles with his backside..."

And at the same instant that he concluded the last wish, the hare with the pink collar, the lamb with the tinkling bell, the white blackbird and the yellow-red-blue-green rat scented with musk like a fog all appeared, simultaneously

"What do you want, Monsieur?" said all four at the same time.

"To go to see my sons-in-law, with this pretty child, who is my dear Houssihoussa."

"That's possible," replied the laconic orator Iouriri, on behalf of the four ambassadors, "but on one condition: this good woman is younger and prettier than Marquise Hhûeip, Duchesse Hhûhhuip, Princesse Bizizbizibizi and Queen Hhouiphhouip, her daughters, which is capable of making all four of them fall in a faint, and even die of suffocation. Now, you wouldn't want to leave as orphans very nimble little green dogs, well-toothed little yellow wolves, well-spurred little blue cocks and well-horned little red sheep, all very lovable and your grandchildren; so, if you want to see them, it's necessary that you both return to the age you ought to be."

"What!" cried Houssihoussa. "I'll be fifty years old!"

"What!" cried Brancabanda. "She'll cease to be young and pretty!"

"Come on," said he laconic muskrat Iouriri. "Decide; destiny grants you twelve seconds and two-thirds to deliberate, but the time lost will be without return. One, two, three, four..."

"Let me see my dear children, but let my dear husband alone remain young!" cried Houssihoussa.

"Let me see my dear children again, but let my wife alone remain young" cried Brancabanda—for both spoke at the same time.

"Oh," Brancabanda went on, kissing his wife, "If you were ten times older now, that impulse of material tenderness and conjugal love would always render you cherished..."

Young, they threw themselves ardently into one another's arms; they embraced tenderly at the age of thirty; they pulled apart in order to look at one another with a tranquil satisfaction at fifty...and all that happened in eight seconds and two-thirds.

Scarcely had the good fellow and his good wife made their choice, however, than a loud noise as heard. It was a beautiful chariot, which arrived *brrrum-brrrum*, drawn by unknown monsters, guided invisibly by the noble Fay of Courtenay, the great Ouroucoucou, protectress of Grignotine, who had rendered the entire family ugly.

Now it is time to say that Grignotine was a beautiful lady and that her children were as beautiful as the day when they came into the world. One day, when the beautiful lady was strolling in the covered path of the wood of Courtenay that led to La Loge, holding on her beautiful white breast her fourth daughter, whom she was nursing, she heard hands clapping in the air. The beautiful lady was afraid, beautiful as she was, and defenseless, when a harmonious and sonorous woman's voice called to her:

"Isabelle!"—that was Grignotine's real name—"Isabelle!"

"What is it, Lady?" said Grignotine slightly reassured.

"It pleases me to see you nursing your daughter, kissing her over and over, like a good mother. Have you nursed your four sons and your other three daughters?"

"Yes indeed, invisible lady—for I cannot see any trace of you."

"You have made a fine gift there to your noble husband! Does he cherish it?"

"Alas, Lady, Pierre cherished me a great deal and I loved him like my eyes, but he has gone to be a warrior, and has left me alone with his living portraits, whom I kiss over and over, incessantly."

At those words the invisible lady sighed, saying: "The battlefield is only better cultivated by loyal husbands whom their wives cherish! Pierre was valiant."

"Oh, Lady, and he is, I still believe, and will be, as long as he draws breath."

"Yes, yes, he has glory, and it radiates like the setting sun of a beautiful summer's day, which dazzles the onlookers who encounter it, but he is no longer alive..."

At that unexpected statement, Isabelle uttered a cry, and fell in a swoon, but without crushing or letting go of the little child. The invisible lady summoned a chambermaid, who was following with the other children, for Isabelle had gone a little way ahead in order to think, over and over, about Pierre, while holding the tender fruit of their most recent love. And the chambermaid brought help to her mistress.

When Isabelle had recovered somewhat, he invisible lady said to her: "Console yourself, my daughter; I am Ouroucoucou, the noble Fay, your godmother. Ask me whatever you wish and I will do it for you, except for the life of your noble husband, which is not in my power."

"Oh, I only want that," cried Isabelle. "I don't want anything else, except to die."

"Aha!" the Fay said, angrily. "You say that you love your husband, and when only half of him is dead, you want to abandon the other half, which is alive, and has no other recourse but you! You would leave these beautiful children poor orphans, then, who would go to live among strangers, and when it is cold, and people huddle around the fireplace, they would remain behind, ashamed, blowing on their fingers. And people would talk to them rudely, and the children of the house would pinch their arms without them being able to avenge themselves, and when the children of the house have honey or jam on their bread, yours would only have walnuts or dry bread, and it would also be heavy. And everything bad that the others have done, it would always be your children who had done it, and would be punished for the others, and treated as bad lots, and they would shed as many tears as they would eat crumbs. Would you really have the heart to abandon them—to abandon the sons and daughters of your friend Pierre, who cherished them and caressed them so much?"

Isabelle was suffocating with tears, and made no reply. But she embraced all her children. "Your noble father..." She could not finish. She started again ten times: "Your noble father...," but a sob was always found in the passage, which stifled the words.

"Isabelle, my dear Isabelle," cried the fay, "ask me what you will, and I will grant it to you immediately."

"O noble fay, what can I ask of you when nothing any longer has value for me? But don't get angry, for...Pierre...I still love his children...and I would still give them what I have of such good and tender love for him, if...if... I'll make you my request, noble fay... Since it us thus, that my dear children will no longer have their generous father, to instill them with all sciences and virtues, I only have one wish, noble fay, and that is that they be good, just, courageous, grateful, faithful, humane toward everyone, as Pierre was... With that, they will no longer have lost anything; for wealth is nothing, at the price of goodness... And as for my daughters, may they be modest, sage, reserved, laborious, economical, meek, submissive and complaisant toward their husbands...with that they can do without all the rest."

"Oh, Isabelle," said the fay, "your wish is fine and good, and I approve of it with all my heart, but the means are difficult, and will perhaps be disagreeable to you."

"I shall accept them. If Pierre...were alive...he would be sufficient for everything, but a poor forsaken widow..."

"I shall act, then," said the invisible fay. "But don't complain; what I shall do will preserve you from importunate researches, and will permit your children to acquire peacefully all that you have sagely requested for them."

As she spoke, the fay showed herself holding on leashes for beasts: a green dog, a yellow wolf, a blue cock and a red sheep, and hidden beneath the face of a little wrinkled old woman from Le Croixpilate, named Grignotine, who had disappeared seven years before with four sons and four daughters. Now, that Grignotine was the fay herself, who sometimes showed herself with one face and sometimes another, to aid the good and punish the wicked. And at the same instant, the noble Isabelle, who had the bearing of a princess, became a little wrinkled old woman, and her children, as handsome and beautiful as the day, became, boys and girls alike, caliborgnon, ratatinet, hare-lipped and disfigured. And everyone who saw them said: "Alas, chagrin has caused Isabelle and her children to die, but Grignotine has come back in their place. We had the beautiful and the good; now we have only the good; God be praised!"

But there came a day when Grignotine, only seeing her children become uglier as they grew older, was exceedingly dolorous, and said to herself: "Alas, alas, what would the noble Pierre say, who was so handsome, if he saw his poor wife and his dear children? He would no longer know them..."

As soon as she had said that, she heard the harmonious and sonorous voice of the invisible fay, which said to her: "Isabelle! Isabelle!"

"What is it, lady?"

"You plaints are not just, but they are excusable. I can make you see by an example what might have become of your children if I had not veiled their pleasant and natural faces under a disagreeable and gross envelope. There is, not far from here, at Charmelieu, or the Red House, a family that I also protect, but secretly—for it has the same origin as yours, and I hope one day to reunite you—all of whose children were born beautiful. I left them their good looks, and you shall see the effect."

Having said that, the invisible lady withdrew, for nothing more was heard.

Isabelle was joyful, and consoled herself for everyone's ugliness, only occupying herself with raising her children well, rendering them good, and, as they were ugly, no one spoiled them, and everyone told them their faults frankly, when they had any.

Now let us return to the arrival of the great chariot.

"The charm has just been broken," said the invisible fay Ouroucoucou, in her harmonious and sonorous voice, and everything is going to be restored to what it ought to be. Your foolish ambition, Père Brancabanda, and your pride and vanity, Mère Houssihoussa, blinded you to the point of having scorned the necessary occupations of a good cultivator of the fields who nourishes the world and make you prefer, for your sons and your daughters, the condition of idlers who desolate it. But I have not abandoned you to yourselves and I have chastised you, because I love you, because you are my blood and you descend from the women of a noble fay family that was once allied with men; as the Grignotins, whom you treated with so much scorn, are descended by the male line, which will determine that you are going to obtain what you have so ardently desired.

"Know, however, that neither your male nor your female cousins are at all deformed but of a perfect beauty, attached to my blood. It is me who has given them, since childhood, a disagreeable envelope, in order that they would be modest, that they would acquire virtues, and that they would not allow themselves to be spoiled by flattery. And it is also me who, in order to cure your daughters of the arrogance that you had inspired in them, made them ugly. It is me who, to correct your sons of their petulance, which is only a superficial vice and not of the heart, rendered them uglier than their cousins that they had scorned; and in that state, they have neverthe-

231

less been loved by the generous daughters of La Loge. It is me who has determined that he Grignotins, so harshly refused as men, abducted your daughters as a dog, a wolf, a cock and a sheep. But that appearance was only for you; at the instant when the dog took Hhûeip by the throat, she found herself in the arms of a handsome, well-made, respectful and tender young man. It was the same with the wolf, the cock and the sheep; and each of them has always seen your daughters with their natural beauty. Here are your sons and your daughters-in-law, and your daughters and your sons-in-law, with the false Mère Grignotine, the virtuous Isabelle, the widow of the noble Pierre, who loved you and obliged you all once— do you recognize her?"

At the same time, an invisible hand waved the faithful wand, which was seen to fly on its own into the air to the great chariot harnessed to monsters. First to emerge from it were four handsome men, taller and more handsome than Sacripar, Fandipouf, Sarôdor and Craquoman, who were giving their hands to four beautiful women: Fidèle to the beautiful Hueip; Belledent to the beautiful Hhûhhuip; Ardentin to the beautiful Bizibizibizi; and Douxregard to the beautiful Hhouiphhouip; leading on leashes beside them the living skins of the green dog, the yellow wolf, the blue cock and the red sheep, which had served them as envelopes.

The faithful wand rose up a second time and struck the chariot; and four Beauties emerged from it as tall and girls of twenty-five but whose physiognomy only announced five or six; each one called to her husband in a little silvery voice. "Come on then, my dear Sacripar...," said the eldest; "My dear Fandipouf...," said the second; "My dear Farôdor...," said the third; "My dear Craquoman...," said the youngest; "...come and see your poor parents, who have missed you so much-for our sisters are waiting for you with their husbands, not daring to pass before you, who are the sons to the house by name and arms..."

And the four sons of Brancabanda, taller and more handsome than ever, leapt out of the chariot and came to embrace their father and mother, each having the skin of an animal around his neck.

"I was the hare with the pink collar, Father," said the eldest.

"And I the lamb with the tinkling bell, Father," said the second.

"I was the white blackbird," said the third, "of which here is the skin around my neck to prove to the world that they exist."

"And I the laconic yellow-red-blue-green muskrat," said the youngest. "After which...after which..."

"Leave it, leave it, laconic orator Craquoman," said the invisible fay. "All the past must be forgotten."

The wand, conducted by the invisible hand, rose up a third time to strike the chariot; and a beautiful lady emerged, still youthful, although she was a good eighty years old, who came to embrace Houssihoussa, said to her: "Do you recognize me, Cousin, and do you want to refuse me your daughters?"

"Oh, Lady Isabelle wife of the noble Pierre de Courtenay," said Brancabanda, "it is a consolation to us not to have been proud without reason, since we are of your noble blood!"

Isabelle smiled as she replied: "Pride is not a vice, but arrogance is, and you no longer have it. The noble fay has taken care of your daughters, and I of your sons. See whether the tender amour of the daughters of my noble husband Pierre has rendered the unhappy.

Fleurdelis, my eldest, cherishes Sacripar; Jacinthe my second, adores Fandipouf; Roserouge, my third, is passionate about Farôfor, and Violetteblanche, my youngest, only breathes for Craquoman."

The faithful wand rose up a fourth time, and young children emerged from her chariot, girls and boys, so beautiful and so handsome that one might have thought them Graces and Amours, who all came to group themselves around their mothers. Brancabanda and Houssihoussa quivered with joy on seeing a good ten of those beautiful children around each of their daughters-in-law and daughters.

"Now embrace your children and grandchildren," said the invisible fay. "Houssihoussa, in preferring to see them again to youth and beauty, has merited the pleasure of living with them and enjoying their respects in her old age... Isabelle, my dear daughter, and you, Masters of the Red House, live happily in the bosom of your families. As for me, I'm returning to the land of the fays; but I shall return sometimes among humans, as an old woman, to test young libertines who scorn the good people of times past, to protect the unfortunate and humiliate the superb. And if you have need of me, here is the ivory talisman; you must do three good deeds; then you should rap on the threshold of your door, and I shall appear immediately. Adieu, my children; you shall see me as I am."

As she finished those words, the fay Ouroucoucou appeared, as brilliant as the Sun. She mounted her diamond chariot, drawn by peacocks with deployed tails, from which she poured a thousand blessings on the reunited families of Courtenay and Charmelieu. Then she went into a big cloud, which the winds pushed, taking with her the ogres of Vaucharme, from which she freed the world forever; and it is since that time that here have been none of them anywhere, nor green dogs, nor white blackbirds, the noble fay not pretending that the latter exist, since her relative had been one.

After the departure of the noble fay, the eight households lived closely united at Courtenay, at La Loge, and at Charmelieu, and they left three fiefs to their children, whose posterity are still the fairest of face and character in the entire canton.

www.ingramcontent.com/pod-product-compliance
Lightning Source LLC
Chambersburg PA
CBHW060356030726
47497CB00003B/728